I0749282

THE CURE

Also by John Fraser and published by AESOP Modern Fiction:

Animal Tales
Behaving Well
Best Friends
Black Masks
Blue Light / Starting Over
The Case
Confessions
Down from the Stars
The Ends of the Earth
Enterprising Women
Exploring the Clouds
Fake Fur
The Future's Coming Everywhere
Happy Always
Hard Places
An Illusion of Sun
The Magnificent Wurlitzer
Medusa
Military Roads
The Observatory
The Other Shore
People You Will Never Meet
The Red Bird
The Red Tank
Runners
'S'
Short Lives
Sisters
Soft Landing
The Storm
Strangers and Refugees
Thinking Scientifically
Thirty Years
Three Beauties
Tomorrow the Victory
Unsteady States, Vol. I
Wayfaring
Wisdom

THE CURE

John Fraser

AESOP Modern Fiction
Oxford

AESOP Modern Fiction
An imprint of AESOP Publications
Martin Noble Editorial / AESOP
28 Abberbury Road, Oxford OX4 4ES, UK
www.aesopbooks.com

First edition published by AESOP Publications

www.johnfraserfiction.com

A catalogue record of this book is available from the British Library.

First edition 2022

ISBN: 978-1-914938-06-1

CONTENTS

THE CURE

THERE'S a little conclave. How to react to illness that might not be terminal.... You have to face the person restored – think of them, probably for the first time, as objects of convenience, desire, loans, or trips to the woodlands or the races.... They say it's a prosperous place here, where the friends live and compete, thriving though many many others there are scrabbling poor. They're a little bourgeoisie that links career hopes to ideas of progress, altruistic friendships, even when the friends are prickly, even boring and obsessed.

'Jarrett sent a message,' Jenny says. 'He's sick, so there's no sense in it, or him.'

'If patients don't have what everybody has,' says Silke. 'They're incommunicable.'

Dagmar's worried. 'Not saying what they have. That's the mystery strain they can pass on. Then you become the mystery.'

'It doesn't sound attractive,' Sarya says. 'You have to visit them, just don't listen to what they say, don't eat their food. No flowers – just donations please. They all say that.'

'Oh come on, Sarya,' Jenny says. 'They're not ghosts – they're just unquiet. They don't all die. I mean, they do.... They communicate, bang on, sentimental. Messaging: those are urgent – heavy stuff; they can't rest until they drop their load.'

'No visiting,' says Silke. 'He won't cure, and we might die of him.'

'At last,' says Dagmar. 'I always thought it was insane, to say people were sick through their own fault. But lately, it's been coming true – not just booze and fags, but walking up and down, taking the bus ... coughing.'

*

Jarrett's message:

'Men and women, lying separately: narrow beds in a long room. A ward: ward like wards in a lock, all locked in our desire. Sick with it, incurable. For me – desire is food. Desire – for love, sex, adventure – is always with us. This is different, the real thing. Food: my desire – its texture, taste, smell. Desire – the keenest prick: the yearning. Food: resist! resist satisfaction, resist the end of desire.

Desire is 'not eating', a purity that lies in 'not eating'.... A long room, full of tiny beds, men and women who hallucinate. Sometimes, I dream.

Those cherries, those olives – stoned. We're all stoned. We don't desire other people's desire – that's meaningless ... but if we were what we think we are, connected, desire should seek desire. But we don't desire other people, them or their desire, we don't seek anything. All's in us, our desire.

There's the time of history and the time of logic, reason. Do they intersect? Ride awhile on each other? And scoot away, on different tracks.

There's another time – the time of desire. Maybe another, too, after that; getting better, losing our desire. Every day, and every way, I want less and less. More desire.

Lots are dying – it doesn't hurt a bit. That's what desire does to you. Drives you, drops you.

More people laid out in the same beds.

The last words – 'oh no'! If the chemicals would let us, those would be what everybody says. Those pills would cost a fortune on the street. Here, we don't pay for them, but they're no fun, bring no tranquillity.

Nearly the last words: you get to say a scrap – love: philosophy ... a making peace, and sometimes war. You get to say your epitaph, but then you have to die....

Pink and scarlet poppies, bunches of them in my head.'

*

'You're looking for a reason, Jarrett,' Dagmar says. 'That's not on the order of the day. Centuries ago, they tried it – maybe you'd offended God, had bad hygiene, were poor and undeserving – or it was a chance for you to think of things malign, benign, and ultimate. Now – it's science. Science gives no reason for a human use. It's quite mechanical – you suffer what you have because it happened to you ... nothing more. If ... then: no motive, no reason.

'Now, you want a motive – political; or a cosmology. It cannot be. We're back to luck – bad luck you got it, good luck you didn't die.'

'You didn't visit me,' says Jarrett. 'Though it's true, I didn't want to see you....'

'We were your friends,' says Dagmar, starting to lose patience. 'We didn't want what you had, but of course, we *are* your friends, for ever, even if we never meet again. Then too – sick people are no fun. They're closed and self-absorbed. Who wants an hour or two of that?'

'I can imagine how I caught it,' Jarrett says. 'We walk beside other living things – our life is made of that. Usually, they are indifferent, sometimes they love us, sometimes they kill us. Try to.

'In my life, there was a puzzle, the puzzle of our century; its politics. It presented you the option: joining in or copping out. Your fate – was similar, whatever you might choose. Pure luck. If you chose the joining in, there was the slow grind and toil – or rush of blood. Spontaneity. The good, the irreproachable, the honest action – simple people, acting Left: trade-union consciousness at best. Then, keenly argued, there was the reason why the spontaneity stalled; there must be: organisation. The grind. A party, discipline. The line. Consciousness. Consciousness of the need for organisation and the line. You would say it's strategy. But the myth, delight – is with our instinct, imagination. It's been hard not to celebrate spontaneity, so long as it was of the left. Hard too not to value organisation. Even a hunting party has it.'

'Well?' asks Dagmar.

'You need both,' he says. 'Probably. No one knows, because it always turned out bad, whatever way you tried. But, I call them sides, in conflict, as that was mostly what they were.

'On the whole, for me, it was the party, though I didn't like being in it,' Jarrett goes on. 'Group, movement, tendency – a line of questioning, of seeing. But all that's past. Quite irrelevant. Not the one and not the other. What I found, when I was sick – all I had left was my desire. Insatiable continuity, in a life devoted to its contrary: turning everything on its head.'

'Did it hurt?' asks Sarya. 'Inside?'

'They hook you up, so you are someone else,' he says. 'Dope. To stop you ringing on the bell.'

'You're antique,' says Dagmar, thinking about politics. 'Your lesson has been learned – it's been synthesised, not to make things change, but just to make things work. We're out of your heroic, awful phase,

Jarrett. Think of something new. Maybe illnesses are old thoughts – you must suffer them, expel them – or they'll kill you.'

*

Remember – the generation of these friends – that fabricates new needs and sells communications, administers the taxes, straightens roads, makes sewers – finds the humble guys to dig, to hook things up, to dispossess and jail – that generation ... it's the fat goose that wriggles into safety, into the hen house as the fox arrives.

*

'Were you just travelling round?' Silke asks me, not absorbed in answer nor in question.

'Breaking horses on the steppe,' I say.

'And left a family,' she says. 'You'd need a bunkie. The nights are cold.'

'So are the days,' I say. 'You can work incessantly....'

'The factories where they make drones....' she begins to ask, raising a painted eyebrow.

'For little spats,' I say. 'They're hunters' shots. The herd proceeds indifferent. Losses don't matter if you don't count them. The instincts are not touched. Always onward.'

'It's good you're briefly back,' she says.

'It's not that I don't trust,' I say. 'I won't commit, that's all. And you're the best of all, Silke, of all your little bunch.'

'I don't ask for things,' she says. 'You and I, we don't need trust. And I've a partner – so don't commit, my friend! I don't.'

'You didn't want to interrupt Jarrett,' I say. 'No disturbance. I might think – you didn't want to know, to verify: that nameless sickness – was he the only one, or were there millions sick and never diagnosed? You make a radical conjecture, but leave it at that.... I don't believe any of you went a metre with him.'

'He was pickled in himself,' she says. 'Desire! As if he was the only one. It's dull. And you, Alex – out on the steppe – the most ancient, enchanted place that's left – but you were anxious, came back here, maybe the safest place there is, but where a thinking person knows – why elsewhere is now silent. All is falling down.

'Here we talk among ourselves, but from all over – no one speaks to us, or knows our names, still less who we all are. And silence will come here too.... And if you stay, you'll squirm. You'll suffer more because you have the info. You left the horses....'

'When I needn't,' I conclude. 'There were troubling aspects there, and bad ones here. But you're wrong. Bad things can be repaired. It takes your energy, you can't be fussed. I return so's I can leave again. Go somewhere else. Think of you, sophisticated and clued up, untouched, untouching. It's meaningless. It reassures – but not for long.'

'Nothing with you's for long,' she says. 'You wish it was. You know it never is, not even on the steppe. You maybe saw how it's illusion – more and more's administered, fenced in. And more and more's precarious.'

'You're right again,' I say. 'I came here when I heard Jarrett was dead, and now he's not, I can congratulate – and leave, relieved.'

'Family,' says Silke. 'A bad sign. It's all we feel a duty for. Alex – your chain is very short – the only link is Jarrett. He didn't mention you.'

'He's right,' I say. 'Though it's trivial. Desire is everything we need. You, Silke – desire is at your brim – your face made up, probably the rest of you, biography, curriculum – except I can't get near enough to rub it off, your story....'

'Why ever would you want?' she asks, amused. 'You see a picture, but prefer the canvas that it's on? You're a collector, and you want the object you desire to move towards you. It's not so. You must bid if you want anything – I'm in the auction that the world is in. Now – will you talk to Jarrett, since you're here?'

'Oh,' I say, 'we broke off, years ago. He can't stop being father, nor I, son. We don't get on. I'm pleased he lives, that's all. It gives me time as well – when parents die, you don't know how the clocks are set.'

'Desire,' says Silke. 'If you have no person, and no place – what can it mean? Jarrett had people, knew where he was, even in his ward.... You have no person and no place, Alex: for you, desire's a desire *for* something. Rather than nothing. You'd be a dreadful companion....'

*

Silke doesn't follow fashion, but she knows what fashion is. That's a catastrophe for anyone she's with.

Silke's much too clean, abrupt, offhand, for me.

Sadness used to be attractive – you should talk about it, spread it around. When the world is Han, there'll be no need for that. We foul our nest – that's why we fly, wings are the gift – if you fly too near the sun, they don't fall off – forget the warning. Forget all the warnings – they came too late, everything comes too late.

You're the best there is, Silke, I can't accept you, can't stand you, and it's reciprocal, we know it without talking, not a word. Sweet as a greengage, much too sweet and sour for me, too mature for almost everyone.

*

'Silke's a beautiful woman,' Dagmar says. 'I can't say that to her face ... her face, if that's not beautiful, is at least symmetrical, the part that must validate the whole.

"Beauty" has been enhanced, multiplied, then fractured into crumbs of time and culture. Something to be wary when you speak about it.... But – I don't find her attractive. Should beauty attract? Maybe it's something in me ... some perversity, a lack, a stereotype. Or is it that her character might not be beautiful? That's really an archaism ... "a beautiful character", went out of fashion centuries ago. Always character was a compensation, but – rather a noble thing to have. At any rate, it seems you don't fancy her, but could desire ... not being eager to attach your projects to her....'

We laugh. Dagmar's a thinking type, seems to fold you in to her concerns, wears woollen leggings, a bandana. 'Silke, I could desire,' I say. 'Not want. It was for Jarrett's death, not her, I'm here – I thought his death would give a jolt, perspective ... a satisfaction of some kind. But – Jarrett lives, and everyone can stay in place, with their old hierarchies.... No need to pull the statues down, deface the coinage, organise parades.'

'We're the top, it's true,' says Dagmar. 'Humans, and people of the free will and judging sort, like us, this little band of friends. Some things must be set out, though. We humans are our own predators. Our camouflage – is lies. Arrogance and pretension help: – but basically, we falsify communication. Find an undergrowth, melt into it. All falsity. Invisible as to what we are, our lies make us an Other. Even if it's just to be a liar – that's enough, it makes us rock or stump, a bole, or tangled leaves. The lie. It's our protection, our salvation.'

Dear Dagmar ... could be my young mother, elder sister, and make me far far out, like her, streaking ahead, past the modern and contemporary, smash into the 'post' – and past the post, a natural platinum, white jade, friend of shades and spooks, cutting a disc with shadowy guys who turn up everywhere in lists of one-offs, who cut scores of discs, wreck cars, sue impresarios, are pure as chrome or nickel, obsessive house-cleaners, bores and minimal.

*

I think of Silke's eyebrows. Am I her predator? Maybe the challenge I took on – horses – wasn't so brave. After all, they're herbivores, no need to cover up for them, they won't eat you....

My lie is – I'm a site: a place, a story, history. Not widely known, so, you can say, and be, just what you want – no questions, and no contestations. There's a distance, then indifference.

I believe my lie profoundly, it is me. My pelt, my furry skin.

Do the horses think they're free – and put in chains? And that one day they'll be free again; do as you're told, they'll trust you – then you can run off, join the herds.... You can't see them, but they're there; on TV you see them, a month's gallop past ... the scene already in the can, everyone gone home.

Too bad – I see them all, the distances.

How patient the villagers were, how full their lives, and how they apologised for being there, the small low houses faded blue and green, scattered like antique boxes fallen off a cart, long long ago, not missed, not put in rows.

I think of Saodat, the Syrian, who said, 'Load the fire of belief on to your disbelief. You must burn. Without death, pleasure and suffering are meaningless. If you didn't grieve for your father when he died, in twenty years you'll start to miss him, and there's nothing you can do....'

All true, like all folklore, and it was her lie. She wanted to be modern, in a modern country, like they used to be, with clean lives lived openly in the street, no need for money, all taken care of, so all you'd need do was work like you did everywhere, all day and night, hefting stuff and broiling stuff, but eventually it had some point. Not that it ever ended.

'Not *in* the street,' she laughs. 'Seeing the streets! The people: so it can't be LA: *that's* all cars.'

'You're destined to be Garbo?' I ask. 'Vienna: "The Joyless Street".'

'Oh,' she says, 'anywhere. Anywhere with streets.'

*

'I do some work with Syrians,' Dagmar says. 'Many were tortured. They don't tell. Some were on what people here say were wrong sides. They don't tell either.'

'Why don't they say?' I ask.

'No one's interested in torture. Nor in why you get enrolled. What good would it do?' she asks. 'Suffering for it another time?'

'How did they get away?' I ask.

'People get tired everywhere. Some prisoners die, those that don't, get out. Same with the soldiering – it's fluid,' she says. 'How you die, how you get out – it's a story if someone writes it, otherwise, it's your life. No one keeps a score. There's no long description. It's what you hear from people who don't talk. I told you, it's fluid. Mostly you want to avoid that. In this country, always the water and the fire come in, change the shape, the faces, but it's like jello, it re-composes. The shocks can be made history. When I say it's fluid – it doesn't make anything, it falls apart, it doesn't make a new shape, it makes sketches thrown away. There's no plot, no characters. No point of view, no one knows what's the meaning of what happens to them.'

It sounds true, plausible.

I say, 'I didn't know you could re-set jello.'

She's impassive. 'That's because it starts off in a pot. If it's in the wild, no, it just runs.'

'Sensibility develops,' I say. 'They say 'strong as horses' – but no one is. I wish I hadn't touched them: your beguiling skills – it leaves you with a fear....'

'If you're afraid of us,' says Dagmar. 'It's only paranoia. I'll rule out misogyny. We carry out the orders – on the whole, we'd rather leave everybody as they are. Like horses. But, we lodge together, each of us has Saodats or Shamsiddins, trekked from afar, we're all in temporary camping grounds – we flock around a well, a pond, and when it dries, we move, or stay and putrefy.'

'It's Jarrett, Dagmar,' I tell her. 'He had the hallucination. What if he comes after me – should I carry? – gun, or knife? He sees us all in beds, lying there, moribund or hollowed out, and dead. He could attack the quick, the ones who writhe and cry – and terminate us all....'

'The feeling's normal,' Dagmar says. 'We're faced with problems much too big to solve and mostly not our fault. And there: the monster comes! A Jarrett, in a smock, a burnous, coming after you with revelations, maybe a new faith, believe: or it's the worse for you. Start counting! Ahura Mazda – will come to earth in several thousand years ... Hindus will wait a much much longer time before the coming and the end. The sickness – belief in the ineffable, gives you the choice. The Christians only have to die, and there's the buffet, all laid out, with tinkle-tankly music, guys with wings to pour out non-intoxicating wine and offer manna canapés....

'Your little difficulty, Alex? A family problem; employment unsure, and where to spend your time.... It's trivial. A little madness doesn't help, but makes no difference. No one cares about you. You should have stayed out there on the steppe!'

'It's been said before, I know,' I say. 'But do you ever think – what a shit place this universe is? Not the dynamic: continual expansion would be great, if there was good stuff to multiply – but there's not. It's a rocky dustheap – shards and acid baths and swirls of suffocating dust – profusions of the uninhabitable – unstable, toxic ... a treasury of awful spots.'

'Yes,' Dagmar says. 'I and you have often thought, like thousands when the telescopes unveiled the mystery: 'the grand design was made by sorcerers' apprentices with machines: presses and duplicators gone crazed, a biscuit factory that turns out blobs and squirms of stuff inedible, misshaped....'

'But I have better things to do than rage at that. I have ideas I must refine.'

I don't ask which. Time enough, when they are pure; but often in the crucible, after the operation, there's a blackened wick left, that's all. Big ideas – they started small, and end that way, unless they're personal.

*

It's an Italian thing, to meet each day, in the street or in the bar, the person who killed your best friend.

If you live, as Jarrett did, by reason, it's natural to end up with its twin, in unreason. He never liked me – now he clings to me, and I'd be rid of him.

I lived by trust, until my friend was killed; my lookalike, you'd take him for me ... until trust died, and then you live distrusting.

They came from Ukraine, they weren't Ukrainians. In Ukraine, you'll find everyone – there must be some Ukrainians there, who do not leave, who speak Ukrainian – I never met one....

They didn't run, so it seemed they must be seeking something, connoisseurs of being never satisfied. Finding a new, a different, place.

The guy who kills – he, she, may have grievances, a rage against the target – but usually they're acting under pressure, not hunting for the guy they're set to kill, but on commission, for some other problem, far far a history away... A debt, an insult. Courting wrong people, in the wrong way. Or courting in too right a way, too much success, too big a dare. Or not understanding a connection, a situation, relationship, a cousinage, a brotherhood, a piece of business rankling or incomplete ... completed and gone sour. You can't go out and kill the killer back, instantly, besides ... behind them there'll be dozens more, and villages which seemed asleep – you live in them flailing, a fruitfly in a web, the monster spider polishing her legs.... Your first mistake – was making friends with someone who has friends, not knowing who the enemies of friends of friends might be. You cannot remonstrate. It's foolish. You can keep quiet – it's nothing.

*

What is to be done? Nothing.

Start a band, a gang. A band of policemen. Of heavies. Or – be a sleeper. Let it fester, be the lone wolf, padding into an enthusiasm – a vengeance, where you've lost everything but yourself, and the idea. The idea – gets larger, you get smaller. Life – you are indifferent. No joy, no hope. Duty is a hard bitch. Revenge. Conviction, certainty – the test. Plant the bomb, sharpen the knife – you're a boil swollen to the bursting.

And your friend – there's nothing to be done. The dead – you can tell their tale, their fantasy. Dig them up, bury them deeper. They don't know, don't care. You can make more dead, for company.

'It's paradise lost,' says Dagmar. 'I won't tell Silke, or the others – you know all the arguments. I hear you over and over, inconclusive. Maybe the noise of the re-telling – it distracts.'

'I don't think about it all the time,' I say. 'Time makes the past grow small, so small it disappears. I know me! I'd rather go somewhere and not remember it at all.'

'Oh,' says Dagmar. 'You can't do that. It's the most important thing you'll have happen to you – bigger than all of us. Irrelevant to Jarrett. Too complicated for him, too full of characters, of plot, of alternatives. You have to think, puzzle out the responsibilities. It's not something you can guess, intuit....

'It's all about you, Alex – everybody back there will know who did it, how you ran away. They may think you were a part of it – a shady shadow, pleading ignorance. The law admits no ignorance of anything, all are complicit. Under the lens: especially you. As well as vengeful, possibly, you're complicit – in real life, not just for the cops. It's something else to calculate. Running away's another; staying away – another still.'

'Yes,' I say, 'you're right. There's justice. But my friend, my mate – he wasn't all that interested ... Or rather, he wanted to avoid it. Doing justice – you might have to find him guilty, and do justice to lots of others, who might not specially want it either. Not to mention those who bring you justice. They may be more interested in cleaning territories that they feel are full of secrets – secrets to them, but not to those who know them, who invent them; a mixture of bad things and profitable ones.... Cleansing – not justice.'

'And that's another exit from your badgers' sett that you can wriggle from,' says Dagmar. 'I'll let you go, my dear, I can't wait to have you gone, but not before you've had a serving of the truths, your offspring in a stew.... I'm out of it, and Silke too, was never properly in.... Silke's refined. Forget her. Then forget me too.'

'I wasn't here for you,' I say.

It wasn't hard to guess.

'A realm of purity, of justice, and above all – faith in justice. That's the answer,' Dagmar says. 'But it would lead you into trouble – deep and dark. Do you want that? Be the big cheese, and take the rap?'

'The Eurasian steppe, on to the Great Plains,' I say. 'There's everything I prize there, all that interests me – but it resists, it isn't in our world. It isn't geography, it's imagination.'

'That fits,' says Dagmar. 'With what Jenny says. When we were modern, we threw away our mum's antiques, but kept our dad's. We lived in cities, trusted the machines, sat on steel chairs, and science cooked our food. But then – it didn't work. All was obsolete: all had to be thrown away. The bombs – made, re-cycled. We had to change too, with the times. We loved King Ludwig, fantasy, adventure trails – eccentric mechanics, and equality with difference, not just formal legal forms. And now – we discriminate – most things are lies and fantasies except what we believe. Hunker down, and don't possess and don't proclaim – put all you need straight in your ears. No one else should be let in. The world is ending, but we must be very very careful, cautious so that the end's, *our* end's, postponed.'

'I told you, Dagmar – lies are camouflage. They let us protect ourselves,' I say.

'That's what you hope,' she says. 'I can't check anything you say. Nobody can – and if they did, the story changes, is transformed, and maybe you're the murderer, or maybe ignorant of everything, even of what you're making up....'

'It's tough, Dagmar,' I say. 'Women like you attained a special place, and then – too bad! The world comes to an end before you get to sing your song....'

'Jarrett's getting close to Sarya,' she says, brushing my barb away. 'She's the softest touch.... It always happens so – when you've been sick, you plan your nursing comfort for the next occasion. She's sweet and yielding – real nougat. But we're all hit by dusty winds – invisible barrel bombs that's landed streets away. Our life's not changed, but where we stand, we've all got smaller recently....'

'There's two types of person in the world,' I say. 'You and Silke. Silke – is onward. Dagmar – you're upward. But everyone's more interested in Jarrett – symptoms and survival ... in Jenny moving in with him, being his heir, enjoying rich old age alone. You and Silke, you are types – Jenny is the person who breaks the bank, carries it off. She's the story. Otherwise – there is no interest. Not in me.'

'It's true,' she says. 'But there's no type of person in the world like you – who isn't here or there, who should be interesting, because you may revenge yourself in ways you do not know, on people we don't know, for reasons obscure to all of us. Meanders that snake around, longer and longer, more sinuous, more poisonous – you said it, said it yourself.'

'I'm an explorer,' I say. 'I want to know why, not what. What am I looking for – doesn't interest me. I'll find it, or not, and tell you after. The why I bother for: that's much harder.'

'No, much easier,' says Dagmar. 'Two lonesome cowboys, you and Zorab there, and fixed in that place.... And now – vengeance, or justice? Maybe they're the same, they overlap. Friendship? Is that the key? I don't think so: it's between you and yourself. Justice – things are the same if it's done or not – enough that someone says it should be done. That's all there is to know. That way – it's done, without the gowns and wigs.'

'I told you,' I say. 'It's not about what you say – it's about the doing. Purpose, action. Mostly, what is done could be better not done at all; or done by someone else, would be the same. We're anty – workers, queens and drones. It's which you're born. We should formalise that: – there'd be the priests, the griots, sellers of leather, dyers, scavengers and scribes. What you're born as, not if you're any good at it.

'The question remains – if everybody else is settled, stacked, then: What am I? Will I do something? Or nothing. Why? Where does the detail fit the picture, the big one if there is, or the small one hung round your neck, a miniature, much prized and hidden.'

'Exasperating,' Dagmar says, quite fondly. 'Whether the world ends or goes on, revving up – there's not a place for you. Except there is, and there you are, sat firmly in it.'

'Kovan was the guy who did the killing,' I say. 'My friend's friend. Zorab was my friend. My friend killed my friend. What now?'

'How were you friends?' she asks.

'Zorab showed me how to do the work,' I say. 'How to get other work, how to do that. He covered for me. There was no money in between us.'

'That's how you have friends, they say. No money,' Dagmar says. 'You let him down, coming here when he was dead.'

'Yes, that's how I feel,' I say.

'We're outside all this,' she says. 'Us who were here.'

'I know,' I say.

'We think a lot about ourselves; and others too, but of them – much much less, except to socialise,' she says. 'We do it leisurely. There's accidents, but seldom storms. We have a way of not encouraging those. You could write it all down in letter form, the thoughts. Or messages – seeing as there are no letters now.'

'The less I apppeal to you, Dagmar, as a person to explore,' I say. 'The more I trust you to give me counsel.'

'You are too closed,' she says. 'And above all you want your situation to close you off. It's a *huis clos*: – you've made a fortress that you can't escape.'

A silence. 'I expect,' she says. 'Those distances.

They yield so much, expectant. There's people wanting guides and passage, and traffic of all things ... Turks,

Iranians ... Kyrgiz, and Kazakhs. You'd be in the middle there.... Trade too. You'd all be traders, in a way.'

'They always were,' I say. 'Passing along. Making the journeys possible, even – an enlightenment. And stuff that's precious to someone: it must get through.'

She doesn't speak.

'Horses – to ride and sell; not carrying the merchandise. Others do that, the porterage: machines as well,' I say.

It's all there, in my eyes.

'You can't go back,' she says. 'And oughtn't to be here.'

'That's exactly it,' I say.

*

'Even broken horses,' Dagmar says, 'are stronger than you are. But it isn't life and death. You might live together.'

'You can say that – you're not there. It isn't like that, not at all,' I say. 'The animals – they don't do deals, and mostly, that is all we do.'

'I mean,' she says. 'You don't do well with people. Animals: – some are everywhere, you could try with those.'

'A zoo?' I say: 'Shovelling? Selling tickets? You're wrong about the horses. We give them a history – they don't have one to remember. For them – it's the solitude. Not the breaking so much – it's being on their own, always.'

'Those that must, they bear it,' says Dagmar. 'You'll learn. Loneliness – is nothing, even a blessing.'

'The more presence that you give,' I say. 'The less it counts.'

'Jarrett is off his head,' she says. 'So he's with Jenny. They're a pair, a pair beats rubbish. Sometimes, it's enough.

'I give you what I have, Alex, not what you want. I'm not an emporium.'

'The world is mine,' I say. 'I invent it all. The philosopher was wrong. A showman. He said we exist only through the others, we are made by how we seem to them. It isn't so. We exist for ourselves, no one else makes us. We may be broken, but we are alone. I make up everything I want, whole continents, their history and songs. It doesn't cost, and they don't have to pay.'

'Well,' she says. 'When you find Kovan – be careful with the dialogue. I bet – there'll be a story; explanations, and excuses. You'll have another friend – a classic. "Friend of your dead friends". Will there be a reckoning, a final scene? I double up my bet: no, there won't be. It's all happened and been resolved.'

*

Jarrett? He's chosen his position – horizontal; and his thoughts – are horizontal too. Jenny takes care of him, then sends him to seclusion, and sells his house. There's a heap of cash. Silke gets some, Sarya says no, she doesn't qualify, and Dagmar says it's a disgrace, but in the end she takes a share, from love of Jarrett, if he'd only been in harmony with reason and with consequences – and from love of Jenny, and of Silke. To pass the benefit around dilutes the blame, if there is some. Besides – what would Jarrett do with cash, when there is nothing he could buy?

Jarrett was cured, before he died. He infected all of us – some don't feel anything, others – don't know what they've got. Some hallucinate, some take dope instead. Each has different symptoms, but we all feel we have the same disease. We all die, but not now, some avenged, some wronged, some for ever avid.

'When I see people,' Jarrett says, 'I see them as if they were cadavers. Sitting at tables, spooning their *tiramisù*. Dead, but not buried.'

How he, and his illness, desired – to signify. Only then can someone take advantage of you … if you signify.

*

We stick together, we feel we must, that it's a need, probably a basis for morality, at least for ethics. We meet the others by happenstance, or in a family we're stuck with treacle or with glue. And so – we are complicit. We make allowances, make arbitrary judgements. Usually, we come out top. We suspect, censure, mistrust – but also want, desire. The free agents are the sick: then, you are alone, yourself, individual in mind and body, fear for yourself. But – you're sick! Out of the game, maybe a moment and you're dead.

That's when you see there are rules, enforcers too, that cluster round the sufferer. How to respond? Adhering to the rules? Judgement won't come for you, but you can do it on the rest. Otherwise – it's complicity or doubt.

SERBIA: THE LITERARY FESTIVAL: THE PRIZE

'*Heureux qui, comme Ulisse, a fait un beau voyage.*' Joachim du Bellay.

I remember the line from a book about the Balkans. He, Ulysses, made a ping-pong between women, or journey down a pin-table ... mostly it's low scores: common matelots and the steel balls – end in the gutter. In the Balkans, you play a ping-pong between countries – likable, lovable, desirable and gross, grotesque, granitic, crude-hewn, uncandid. Uncompleted wars. Pig wars.

Publishers, foundations – they love competitions: wars, post-wars, attract them. 'Spot the genius, and let us not spend. We have the keys to the dark wood, the coppice, spinney, where you'll be lord of owls and weasels. Fame.'

People knowing, not knowing, who you are. Mostly, we can write. I do. I'm a writer, so I ought to have a prize. That's why I'm here.

'Animal Tales' it's called, my submission: you describe your adventure. If they like it – they pay you decently. And print. If not, you get Balkan food – cheese made in a sock, bean soup, dried mushrooms like wood-chippings. The bean soup's my favourite. And expenses, to get you somewhere else.

A lady wins who made incongruous pets. I tell about the horses, not about Zorab. It sounds ordinary and far-fetched.

Anyone from East or South: there's prejudice. No – there's disdain. All we Ulysses ... we lose; no one believes our stretched tales, or twinkles in response to our muted fairy lights.

Then – who gets paid? The temporaries, or the resort hosts? Who feeds us? No one. It's evident....

The sponsors disappear, no one is paid. No expenses, nothing: collapse. Lawyers will come....

Forsaken and forlorn, no Circe, and we losers, are pigs on our own: in nature, we'd be cannibals. Here, we are marooned. Russia? Where might you be? – too far off, too big to help. The sponsors would object. They are not here, but nor is anyone.

Emily – a Basque, a Catalan, a loser, expert in coming second, says 'There's a cheap boat to Italy.'

Her story – she fantasises about camels in the Pyrenees: transgressive; full of goodness, probably.

We're inland: and don't have the fare. 'Emily' – another writer, visionary. A separatist, who knows – if you aren't made president of your piece of folklore, you run a mafia. These little states attract the crawly things. There's capital. Cash in sacks, and comprehension, complicity in scarlet uniforms.

I remember du Bellay, he said, 'Italians are shit.'

'No,' I say. 'We've been made refugees. Everywhere is closed or dangerous. We don't want new life. Our old life's been judged uninteresting. We could go South – they'll understand us there.'

'I don't want understanding,' says Emily. 'I want help.'

'We need a *passeur,*' I say, 'who works for free. A horse – it couldn't jump the walls and fences – and if we were on a sled....'

The snow's quite deep. The horses here look numb – they'd pull us out of deeper holes than this.... But we see no one. The snow spreads out its arms and ghostly hides the landscape.

'No,' says Emily. 'Don't touch me, please.'

'It was a slip,' I say. 'And you, the camels.... They symbolise the people, Moors! But you don't say, don't want. Afraid of offending them, our careless hosts. Your tale's a prank, no more....'

It's the best critique she'll ever have. She doesn't speak.

MAROONED

The winner and her friends – they stayed apart. The locals slipped away – and now, like a snowball, a balloon drifts down, silver and silent. It lifts the winner and her friends. They don't wave.They disappear. They didn't speak to us, they turned away – the winner's snook.

'They flew her in,' says Emily. 'Because she had to win. They fly her out, because she's light. A flake.'

'There's no way of ending this,' I say. 'We're artists, so we don't owe anyone. No one owes us. And we can't write ourselves out of Serbia, not with our two keyboard fingers anyway. Our story ends here. Is anybody reading this? If we don't know what follows – nothing does....'

'It was a mistake,' she says, 'writing about the *Reconquista*. Some pasts the people won't exhume. At worst, there's regret for pleasures lost – bad cess to history! At best – it's making good, and harvesting the cash – like we are trying. Doing things right.'

'You wrote about camels,' I say. 'They don't have faith.'

'Nor do I,' she says. 'But camels can survive, I can't. I need to stir it: it's a cauldron. No matter if it's edible.'

*

Our situation's one of greatest difficulty.

'If we hug together in this stable, Emily,' I say, 'and if a sheep, a horse, warms us with its breath ... we can survive this night. Otherwise....'

'Then it shall be otherwise, Alex,' she says. 'You're strange. A spirit wandering, abandoned. Is it vengeance you want, or peace? You're enigmatic. What happens if we lie separate, and in the morning we'll be found, two frozen cods, and someone, from fear or prudence will find us, ship us out...?'

'You're right,' I say. 'Consequence and causality. Take our two bodies. I remember from my school, how Newton's laws account for Mars's orbit. "In a system of two masses interacting according to an attraction inversely proportional to the square of their distance," he said – and so and so.... Someone will remember how it goes. There you have it! We're in orbit! Each element is essential, but none is the *cause.* We are those masses – distant and determined. We'll be found stiff in the morning, and they'll ship us out – you to Spain, me to Paris. Paris is where they send the unknown artists, in hopes ... of uncertain consequences....'

'Being bitter, Alex,' Emily says, in a huff, 'will not distort my will. Lie in the hay, apart; and hope.'

*

I'm right. We're stiff, refrigerated, like those heads, deep frozen brains, waiting for the resurrection. She's bound for Spain, a part, a moon, spun off. And me to Paris, like I said. I had an address – the Quai Voltaire – in my pocket. My cause.

The Quai Voltaire – a cemetery of books and doubts: – the graves, where you'll find what justice means. Emily's enchanted. Knowledge! What you need to be a politician or a boss. So, here she is.

I'm out of date.

Paris looks that way too.

Jarrett knew about desire: if you don't know what for, and it doesn't matter to you anyway, it's a discovery. Like digging something up, unique. It's a great enterprise, but someone else will have to identify it, make sense, launch it in a contemporary stream. All my doubts and struggles – they're already parts of history that someone else will weave. They have no value, worth, as they stand and as they trudge along. My efforts – harbingers of my mortality.

Kovan, the killer, my friend, my victim. What does morality tell me? 'No! Don't do it. Vengeance is mythology – it doesn't work, it isn't just – and worse, you're next in line to be the victim. Make a friend of your friend's friend. Work something out. That's ethics.'

What do you owe, what's in for you, left you from your ancestors? Nothing. Dagmar ate your father's bones. Don't call for her. Ask Emily. She won't make friends and similars – she'll make a little state, perhaps, and that will make her hop, and sacrifice her friends.

We're artists – we make up our rules. I write for horses who can't read, but they're appreciative.... Listen, Emily –

'The steppe's a realm of freedom. It's always been a market where slaves are traded – black, brown and white, with price lists. And every kind of labour forced, enforced: national or tribal.... Most people in most history have been enslaved, or lived with slaves, lived thanks to them, or felt enslaved – by lords and nations, empires.... There's no vaccination to keep it off you, or protect. That's your project, Emily: finding people eager to be slaves.

'Kovan and Zorab? – a long, long history of being not recognised, not acknowledged and if you are – it's worse. Much worse. Maybe differently, but worse.

You're ripe for culling. Slavery; revolt, then massacre ... some scars are put on you at birth, or earlier, others are acquired through life. Like the branded sheep: as it changes owners, so the branding-iron is modified.... Zorab, Kovan – they were free to run, to work – but when you saw them, you knew they were not whole. Something of them belonged elsewhere, to people, a person, you couldn't see. Or – that didn't exist, not anywhere; like humans, when in the womb the tail is lost. That's everybody's loss – but maybe there is more for some or all to lose or gain – horns, a crest, a shell. A colour, language, suzerain....

'I'm in difficulty. And you are in the service of a liberation I don't credit. Hundreds of groups, thousands of dialects, of people crammed in states and borders – must each have a flag and tax and treaties too? And armies, cops and spies? Enough! It's infinite regression – every band will set out, through the savannah, meeting other bands, hostile or not, forever alert, suspicious.... And each is exterminated in turn, or founds its state, and waits – for its extermination or becoming empire. It cannot be, there must be something else ... not revenge, not justice.... Mine's quite personal, the challenge. Yours ignores modernity; what's changed, what needs confronting. We're all in a sinking boat, each would be the rat, but no one swims.... Help me! I'm alone, you have comrades ... you can't lose comrades, can you – but I'm lost, myself, lost....'

It isn't eloquent. I can't express emotions I don't have – it shows. I need a wall that I can bounce off – Emily is perfect. She's not with me. She shuns help, so did Jarrett, with his desire for what is not. Desire for itself, unfulfilled, for that – to be desired. I need help to find out what I need help for.

'I can't resist,' she says. 'Not that I tried. I hear a soul abandoned, and I prayed. My vision – a mini-state, where we all tramp in step. Money flows in, and we enjoy.... My struggle – it responds to yours. Your Kurds.'

'Oh no!' I think. Maybe some of what she says, she may believe. I say: 'Emily? You'd be a burden, worse than guilt. Your illusions ... keep them to yourself, deal with them as you can ... don't share them, not with me.'

Besides .... it's wrong, she's wrong. Without a state, you don't fight for yourself, you're a proxy, mercenary, deluded, gangs, assassins, martyrs ready for the pyre. Someone else is using you, the little that you maybe get is a tiny part of what you have put in. You need a state – but find then that it doesn't serve. The power – goes to the new class of boss, not to you … I say –

'It's not about a state, not even that – it's about strategy, by states that don't care if you live or die. Big states that skip the little ones across the ponds.

'You choose the biggest friend you can, and it will use you, drop you from the greatest height. You're a chicken – not to lay eggs, have chicks, but for the pot.'

'You have me wrong,' says Emily. 'I pray. I don't have ideals, or politics. People, nations – that was Byron. The flags, the dying. What comes next? Those awful colonels? ... not his type, I'd guess. I want the good part. The relax, the luxury. Alex – you describe the bad: the torment little players end with when they try to beat the pros.

'Not everybody loses – and when the big ones play, there's losers among them there.... If you're not careful, you implode, or get some stupid chief who overplays a hand.... Forget your vengeance – you're clearly not convinced that murder is your thing. Move on! Let's see how we can win, without a fracas, with no gang, no blood....'

'I was a lonely horse,' I say, dismayed, 'looking for someone who'd ride me, give a destination and a destiny. When you're broken, that's the best there is....'

'No doubt,' she says, offhand. 'I'd want to turn your lead into my gold.'

'I don't bring much to market, Emily,' I say.

'You're a distraction,' she says. 'That's useful. Guys like you end up as president. Remember, though – my religion says – "don't practise casual sex".'

'All mine says is "do it, if you can",' I say.

'Cash is better,' Emily says, 'than almost anything. It can be spent on almost everything, including more of itself. Invest. That's what you tapped into, Alex, when you got the horse job – but you didn't see, that little bands and gangs get paid. They're retail. You seem to tread on clouds of wholesale. It's a waste – think big, gain small. That's what they say. And vice versa too.'

'Are you sure that's what they say?' I ask. 'It sounds to me you're just a tyro, seen too many flicks.'

'The writing, Alex?' she says. 'That competition. You get contacts. You get screwed. Your ego's engorged. We both had the lesson, of abandonment. I thought my camels were a delicate touch – but the steer was in! The lady with the balloon; her destiny was to win.'

'It gets cold on the steppe, of course,' I say. 'We could both resist. We're toughened up together, chaste. And I made a structure quite robust – sewing a quilt that held together horses, and my father's hallucinations.... I could be a genius, exploring unknown provinces. Who knows what horses dream? We should have kept some bean soup to warm us up....'

'You see?' she says. 'Your mind's all shreds and cores. If there's no tale, you must tell it straight, as if there was. Intimacy – with sex: or family unhappiness. That's what they want. Anyway, we tried. It was a fix. Too bad.'

'My presentation – it impressed you, then?' I ask.

'As a writer, there's no doubt. You are a genius. I don't say it lightheartedly,' she says, straight-faced. 'I've been told quite frequently, that my version was a work of excellence too.'

'Not genius,' I say.

'There's the nub,' she shouts. 'The product counts, not the source! I accept we're both geniuses, for what it's worth. But my stuff has the edge – strikes to the heart. And yours – meanders, requires explication, a knowledge of fine words and reference.'

'All this, Emily,' I say. 'It doesn't count, or make a difference. To the producer, with dispersion comes no joy. Don't distribute – keep the satisfaction close, reserve it for yourself.'

'Of course,' she says. 'But if as artists we can't collaborate and risk dilution – maybe ... there's fruitful work for each.'

'The Quai Voltaire,' I say. 'It's a good base.'

'But not for art,' she says. 'Perhaps your mother said the poor were criminals. That may be so – but criminals aren't poor. The Quai Voltaire is the plum. Books. Old money. That leads to thoughts of crime, and justice. To me – and you. Stroll from the Quai Voltaire to the police – the Quai des Orfèvres. Go deep and deeper, beyond your speculation – to the cops. The citadels – police, and justice. The law, vendetta, vengeance – what is right and just – and best of all, you don't need do it, not anything at all. No killing, no second thoughts, or first ones either – from the novel to the guillotine. Then – write it down: that's how you thrash things out.'

'I understand,' I say. 'You want to be let in – into the net that strangled my best friend, Zorab. And do what must be done from here, the Quai Voltaire.'

'That's what I'd want,' she says. 'If I can.'

'Jarrett saw us all as corpses,' I say. 'He despaired of me. He wanted me to be an artist, a thinker, not a cowboy. All corpses. And he ended in the hands of those who loved him, and each took a piece of flesh, an arm, tore off a leg or tail, until he was quite right: he was a corpse. Cadaver. Unthinking.

'The truth, Emily, the truth is dross. So are lies; like the Italians. I see things as they are – that's all you need. Why dress it up with fard or kohl? Tragedy and comedy – the masks. Jarrett ran ahead of life – it got him not more life – much less. The lesson wasn't learnt, by him. He cheated – peeked at the final page, and didn't see the volumes following, where he was prey, and dead. Dead meat, and carrion, Emily.'

'You don't know much, do you, Alex?' she asks.

It's quite a surprise, to hear her snip, coming so soon after her ploy to join my crew, my index and my contents list: 'How things work. History. How life is pain and doubtful choices. Curiosity: why people bother with it. Why some sides win and some lose, in the end, how long it takes, and what they live on in the while. When our flash moment will pass, and how someone might repair our damage ... no one knows.'

'I'm not a scholar, Emily,' I say. 'And don't do maintenance. That's for vets and wainwrights. Scholars have to work where they're not seen. On the steppe, you're visible: you must be aware, always alert. You can't escape – it seems it's all escape, in all directions, though everybody sees you run, knows where you are. You never leave, there are no doors and exits, you don't hide.'

'Crap,' says Emily. 'You all were betrayed. Maybe *you* weren't. Someone was: lots, probably – betrayed. Who to? Aha! Your friend, your friend's friend: Zorab or Kovan, on commission, or by the code, kill or be killed, but above it all – be loyal. That's what "friends" means. One seemed to be an infiltrator, a traitor. One was killed as punishment, or sacrifice. One – the same one, or another – was killed to hide the other's treachery. Or was it all suspicion? Who whom?

'Yours is a leaky boat, Alex. That attracts. It's full of treasure. So is making little states – if you get out in time. Clinging to big crumbling states – best stay away from those.... Though if you're smart, you can still take out your cash, and even someone else's....'

*

Emily's a wonder. Not wonderful: a surprise in a long dress.

I put my experiences in order through the animals. A hierarchy, a meaning, the chase chased in gold – lions and zebus – put yourself in their bodies, their jaws, their twisted barley-sugar horns, apparently useless.... That's what they did, the people in the middle, between north and south. Animals don't think too much about us, though. There's no reciprocity, beyond domestic needs. They're like wives and husbands married long ago, left around, planets circling round a cool star – or old flames, like the foxes with brands tied to their tails, gone deep into the forest, crying at night – prey or predator. You hear them, not in the singular, as an eternal question: owl or mouse, a whoo? a meeee!

The universe is harder still: does the moon, do the stars – have a hand in how we grieve, live years depressed, evenings now and then of joy? No. They're in it for the long haul. We're stardust, can be vacuumed. All we are is ephemeral, shades without a substance.

Better, if you feel the need, to project emotions, speculations – as shapes. I think of Silke, Dagmar and the rest, as hills. Emblems of a city, wealthy, long ago in India. The four hills over the river bend, the cities across from one another, and the fish, the wealth: and Jarrett ... clear troubled water, curling coldly round between high banks, troubled by the dodgem race of perch. Hills are familiar, not lovable. Not likeable.

Someone must care for us; at least, about us. Who, if we don't? Our brain is set up so we are all the same. Our disquiet – what becomes of us, we tadpoles in a jar? Uncertainty's an illness. The cure – it ought to be generic, universal, the advice be good for each. It isn't so. Experience – always different, always identical. Emily – it doesn't interest her. Is each of us a pattern, design? jigsawed, scraps of a big picture – a thousand pieces. Reconstitute the wholes, every piece is in the box, one piece missing would destroy the picture: a flat calm sea ... a fire, a landslide, shipwreck ...

Emily's a pro. She's worked out all she needs to think. Thinks better than I can.

*

How do we transgress, crouching on the Quai Voltaire? People must come here to enjoy, when they've been bad successfully.

'Emily,' I say, 'maybe our base should be less ostentatious. Rich guys and arty types abound in symbiosis here.... Remember, we're organising trades we're not supposed.... Each seeks justice – I'm terrified; and you'll betray.'

'Oh,' she says, 'don't worry about money. I'm a success, so I've got lots. And I want more. You get it living side by side with affluents. Cash sticks to the summit, the tall rock: it's like mussels – you need a sharp knife to prise it off.'

'I'm amazed,' I say. 'I'm destitute. My father's hallucinations – they're not saleable. Besides – he's been dismembered. Theft and fraud – I entertained those to reach a minimum, then I could maybe deal in stallions, buy a fur hat, some cowboy boots.'

She laughs, I pull a sad clown's face. 'You quite deceived me,' I go on. 'I thought you were a poor bozo, just like me, knowing, perhaps, some other tricky bozos....'

'No, no,' she says. 'That's cinema, for guys who can't get off the couch. You underestimate me. I once won a prize: my one-act play. I have success in everything I do, or else I wouldn't start. "Beats Brecht and Ibsen" – that's what the judges said. And it is true. It wasn't staged, alas....'

I prompt her with a sign: 'I told you – casual sex,' and she pouts. 'Even from a judge – it isn't on,' she says, twirling her shoulders. 'That industry is worse than arms or aviation – fraudulent, corrupt. Writers and their books – inventing justice, cultivating crime.'

'Entertainment?' I ask, still disconcerted.

'Law,' she says. 'That's where the judges roost.'

'You know the scene,' I say.... 'It rocks ... in a bad sense....'

'It's goods and moving them, consuming some, and others go as pay-off to the boss,' she says. 'What more is there to know?'

'Am I consumed?' I ask. 'Or shall I be betrayed. Hooves, wings and wheels – they're only technical, like bags and boxes. My attributes, like Mercury's. Nothing wrong or profitable in what I've done.'

'Have no fear,' she says. 'I'll take you with me to the top. You'll fly. And if I'm not top bitch in my little state, I'll anticipate my fall, the corruption, coups – and start a gang. Be really bad. And tough. If I can't start a gang, I'll be president – it's easy, normal, in a tiny state. Yes! I'll be a president with a gang. You need executioners and bards. A big state – needs bombing planes. You'll be an honoured guest, my dear.'

'And if I don't want that?' I ask.

'So many people I sent out to do my work are dead,' she says. 'Money is what's left. That becomes your choice, my choice for you: money, or death.'

'I spot a flaw,' I say. 'Where I was, I wanted neither cash nor death.'

'It was a limbo,' Emily says. 'Anyone with courage, and intelligence, gets both.'

'You don't go deep,' I say. 'Even the horse-men – saw the lion will kill, but in the struggle, she and the prey both live intense and dramatically.'

'Deep?' she says. 'All this, what we see, and one day shan't, is deep. An illusion? Every surface rests on depth. In your view, the unknown's deep, you wrestle with it. It's incomprehension – but when it's known, it isn't deep at all – you can play sandcastles with it, a *mandala* you can scatter when it's complete.'

'I can't live like that,' I say. 'Not without an unknown that multiplies.... And your beliefs – all quotes. Used them myself a score of times.'

'What's that to do with all the people we bring here? Our traffic and our syndicate? Our crimes. The mules?' she asks. 'They are unknown, we hope, and they forget what they once were. And all the stuff in plastic parcels. Known or unkown?' she laughs again. 'You'd better know, so you can set the price.'

'Then, it's better mountains than the steppe,' I say. 'Or desert. The unscalable, the mirages … I lived on grass, I was the horse who sees its rider endlessly struck down, and does not raise a hoof in retribution …'

'The flatlands,' she says, provoking, 'may have a world beneath them, but they're not for us. They're for the birds! Venice, those sinking islands, the Deltas – Danube, Amazon; avoid them. The tundra, the swamp, the mangroves – the plain! Well named – the plain, the dutiful, the ending there must be, the tail, the tailings, dribbling down ... grass: flesh, mown, dried and mortified....'

It's true. Armies, horse-borne, vanish, unchronicled, unrecorded. Never registered, peoples who have lost their name, little horses in a string, put a dozen in a box, shake it – and they're gone! Disappeared! It's not a trick, it's a knack.... I once could do it by myself.

*

Everything I know, have seen – Ulysses knew it, saw it, first.

It's a disappointment.

I feel terrible regret, grief for my friend and for my friend who killed my friend. Anger, regret for death.

*

Miguel takes our messages: he's an informer, quite invaluable. 'Do you like my *redingote*?' he asks. 'Red's the colour of my bike as well.'

Emily laughs. 'It's baggy,' she says. 'It'll get in your chain, you'll do an Isidore Duncan.'

'It's a tent,' he agrees. 'They're all over, all over Paris, everywhere. Africa, the Orient – encamped.'

Miguel gives us perspective. Close up, it's traffics – people, money, goods and bads. Influence, contracts, capitals: interest, indifference, playing the market, playing the horses, playing and being serious. Almost everything is here, is everywhere, is legal and not quite: in and out the rules ... making the rules, interpreting them. Getting opinions, arbitrations, settlements, plans to do and plans not plans, plans to don't … Plans to scare, to last for ever –

Emily is good, masterful. So good you know if anyone's to suffer, it is you. She has friends who are not friendly, dislike her, fear her, runners, between Quai

Voltaire and Quai des Orfèvres – cops, robbers, fixers: go-betweens and diplomats.

It's not my thing, none of it; it's life. I distrust it.

Plutocracy, is that our goal? I'm afraid of being caught, even if we are the catchers. It's an alibi, it's no good for making or unmaking what I've made. You want sufficiency, and when you have it, over and over – you've assured a crowd of people that they'll live in insufficiency. It embarrasses, to say that. Everybody knows, the exercise is in not saying it.

'You're a brigand,' Emily says. 'It's a fine life, full of sparks. Enjoy it.'

*

'Maybe you don't belong,' says Emily. 'You can always go back. More pride, less prejudice?'

'You've found someone to do it better than me here?' I ask. 'I'd go back, back somewhere, if it's not been spoiled. Spoiled by me, and you.'

'Listen,' she says, squeezing my ears, ah! her perfumed paws.... 'People who use us, who we use – have done the sum. They must have trust – in mathematics, at the least. Better leave where can't be worse, and take what comes. Maybe they're wrong: it's worse. It's unpredictable, and not our fault. As for the rest – it's venerable. Business. Capitalism – the autonomy of who has cash or swagger. Some in the law, some ... hmmmm. It's not a drama. Small fish are caught and fried – the big fish break the net, and find another stream. Don't take it seriously. Don't cry – no one is moved.'

'My friends....' I start.

'I tried to make you grow, Alex. But you've stayed small: a dwarf. Just like your friends. Beware!' she says.

'I'm in a web,' I say. 'I try to leave, to kick my way out and into something else – but it's my life. I don't want it, whatever it is that happens to me – but that's the pattern of the web, its circles and its centre....'

'You won't reach the centre, Alex,' Emily says. 'It wouldn't matter if you did. I want everything I do, and nothing happens to me I don't want, however hard it is. Besides – your Kurdish friends – betrayed and beaten, and those old traditionalists, those foxy bosses, biding better times.... They took Islam lightly. Now, perhaps, they'll take another path.... They might say – "if your friends are rubbish, why not try your enemies?"'

'I hadn't thought,' I say. 'Maybe. Maybe you try politics and fighting and it doesn't work, so you go round the opposite way.... Cosmology and gardening.

'I just don't know. I've known every kind of militant, each conviction – the steppe flattens it all out....'

'No,' she says. 'Look what happens to you, and those round you. You can't ignore anything at all. Nothing worthwhile is flat.'

'They say it's in our heads,' I say. 'All our thoughts are those devised by white West males – if we just opened up to other worldviews.... even the universe –

must have views …those space-craft have such tiny portholes ….'

'What we do is just the same all over: it's wrong, what they – you – just said. Thoughts are like clouds,' says Emily, 'they're always there, above. Sometimes the East fights wars and feasts on delicacies – at other times, it's us who do the same, exactly. Deeds are the same, like the beliefs – there's variations, but the colour and the place, the sex – is immaterial. A place is brash and feisty for a while, and puffs its profs, its armies ramp around – it doesn't mean a thing. The moment passes – and the strength goes somewhere else. The thought – it drifts.

'We're global, Alex – what we do is called a crime, all our businesses are judged that way – but they are everywhere. All times. No sex, no colour and no place are fixed. It's traffic, trade, free people fleeing, free capital that circulates....

'The transformation that I have in mind would be a source of joy for you, of pride. If we were unisex, with males about to be extinct – you would be rare, and even prized. Your sentimental character would reach its apex! You'd be the last! The source of all nostalgias to come....'

'It's true,' I say, 'India. A man feeds a big gibbon with a fruit, and briefly – their fingers touch.... I wept. It showed....'

'It showed you should be off,' she says, quite brusque. 'We don't need tearful types in our activities.'

She pushes me towards the door, not touching, herding like a collie dog. Behind the tender nose, there's hidden teeth. 'People like you,' she says. 'Who think their doubts and questions find more truth, and give them moral sheen – are wrong. The more you question values – the more they deflate. It's not that they become part of the machine – they disappear. Doubt creates doubt, history creates history, life creates life and death. No one gives a damn.'

That could be true: I doubt because I am confused. I am confused because I don't know where to turn to save myself.... Beyond the door, there is the president, with guards, the assembly and academy, security and hospitals.... They're set against me – even the hospital – best not go in unless potentially you're dead. Potentially – all are. Like on the street, the manif – take a clubbing the wrong way – your life turns upside down – a stone skimmed on a pond, the earthy surface turns upside, and everybody sees – the underside. A pose unseen in life. I think of Jarrett, untired in his bed. No one cures you – you must cure yourself, select the powder and the drip – they're riddles. Choose the wrong one, the wrong casket, the wrong name and label, and you don't get to bed the princess, wear a crown – they bundle you in sheets and when its dark, down the chute with you, into the ditch, the pit. The muddy laundry.

I can't stay here. I must have a destination.

PRAGUE

Can I be a waiter in Prague, the magic city? Yes, of course, in a cellar, nostalgic, the menu of the 1970s, dry roast chicken....beer. Emily – got me the work. I'm not a good waiter. People crowded in, smiling, I didn't understand a word, all I could think of was Stalin. He didn't do an auto, an authorised biog by someone else.

I imagine him, sat here, docile, quite pissed ... memories you mustn't think of.... An Aztec mind – the more sacrifices you make, they keep you safe and sanctified. The more the sacrificed, the holier, the more protected you are, till there's only you left, to hobnob with the deities – that you believe in, or you don't. They let you down. They are dependable, because you never see them. In a big country, the other little countries seem very far away. And small: we're small here. Did he think they'd learn to live here in a better way? I could believe in dragons....

I haven't believed in magic now for many years. We know about him, and his context: history. That's a dolls' house, a model theatre – you can put in giants or midgets – both are miniatures.

In the cellar, there is beer, in huge steins, urine samples from Valhallah, and bats like wind-up toys from fantasy movies, trying to escape the light – up and down under the rough-cast roof. I never saw the magic, maybe it had gone to Turin, another magic city, but if you have two points you can triangulate them with a third that's anywhere, and the magic goes there where'd you never know. Never returns.

Magic is metamorphoses, but those happen to us all, constantly, we flow from egg to cock and cuckoo, dementia to foetus.

All that's left of socialism – is that waiters don't get tipped. Comrades. The only way to make a revolution: a putsch, then the single party and its *shef* become a mafia, and they spread, a colony, a vine, a web lodged in the cellar here ... Up go the prices, and there's awkwardness. There must be other ways, but watch out for Americans, the bankers, and the fickle folk as well. The *nomenklatura*, the system, creeps into us – they are our time and we submit, as trees submit to summer and to winter. All gone, of course, gone completely.

*

I believed. I believe in anything that promises so much that something must remain, even if the sacrifices are unavailing.

It's plausible, that theory.

All this was long ago, but also now; when I try to get away from Emily, and humanistic crime, that does some good to everyone and some bad to something abstract, to friends as well, and naturally, the friends of friends....

'I know. Wild horses – they keep pulling you,' says Sandy, someone I liked, and shall not miss. Sandy, the barman, waiter, hustler. You tell him everything – so what? There's nothing he can do with it, not work it, fashion it to something fine or useful. Just secrets and ambitions – everybody has them – it's backing numbers at roulette. Your number will come up if you persist, but usually the money finishes, or the realism prevails, and so you never know. You've gone; reformed, bitter or unbothered. Like women, when you're straight: – they size you up, and you are wanting, even if you only want a room, a bed, on temporary terms.... Now, everybody's straight, one way or other. It's good; to you – it makes no difference....

'Wild horses, pulling you to where you're sure you never want to go, though still, it's home, or better, it's the stage where you will do all that's special and memorable. And curse you came,' he says.

'The horses – we make them pass from nature into culture,' I say: 'Free trade, along these old roads. The tracks left – for certain, they are culture. So is trade. We have little left now that is nature, not that I'm upset. Trade? It's all for sale, it doesn't seem free to me, but there it is. The money goes to someone, whatever you might call the trade.'

'Almost everything is culture,' Sandy says. 'When there's some nature left, it gets protected. It's shaped and worked on. People pay to see it; there's guys following the nomads, filming. You can't keep making the distinction, identifying nature, if there is no evidence. Do what you must, against nature....'

'Oh,' I say, 'I wouldn't think of it. Breaking's got to be a dirty business – too much money chasing what shouldn't have a price. It always has. That's what the grass, the space, was for – trading the horses, making cavalry, and see it ride on through.'

'If it has a value, it must have a price,' says Sandy. 'My school insisted on it.... But do *you* have a price, Alex? Or a value? The horse does, but you – are replaceable. A part of something, not a whole, not a spirit that inspires ... that's you. You're a soldier, like all working stiffs: you fall, the guy behind steps forward in your place, becomes you, the spandrel that you were....' He concentrates, explodes, goes on –

'*You,* Alex, as you – don't have a value, and your price is exactly what the guy behind will have. The horse, though....'

'It's true,' I say. 'The horse may not recognise the moment of its death, but it knows exactly what precedes and follows it – first, its enslavement, then freedom. Free again ... the minute that you die, unbroken again. So – he, she, will roll on you, and bite, try to break you against the fence, shake you off or run with you until you die of fright ... throw you on the ground and stamp on you. When you're dead, Sandy, there's nothing to remember of you. Your soul – went in to the breaking. You lost it there – so did we all. Horses – are born free, they are reborn. We – are born enslaved. We have no hope! That's why the shaman chants, shoots up: it's consolation. Not for us....'

'The moments,' Sandy says, musing, probably agreeing. 'The kiss, the stab, insertion of the card, buying the flicker, putting in your number, signing on or off – except you do not sign, not with your writing: those moments are decisive. It's a sequence. A moment is nothing, but it brands you, a sheep, with red ochre: keel, it's called. After the moment – the scald – the passage is complete. You leave the people that you know, become citizen of a new ungoverned, rule-thick, world. You're out of nature, sure, it's not offered: but into – what? A company of shades, of ciphers, encrypted wants that you can't recognise. A world of them. You can be illiterate: like kids who recognise the sura from its shape, an arabesque: telling of beads, whirling the wheel, watching the fluttering flag .... all those were a beginning. Then – an interlude, of literacy and uncertainty. After that – a new regime, of symbols, falsities, conventions, a world inhabited by lying gods. You and I, Alex – we've gone beyond the end, and out the other side, beyond discussion, setting out a plan; into a twilight, without sun or moon. It seems we're pioneers, but everyone is just the same – stepping on the new planet, bundled up in white; not communicating.

Terrified and feverish.

'Or hatching in a nest beside cold marbled eggs, your siblings unfertilized....'

'You're lucky, Sandy, you never left this city, you've been always here,' I tell him. 'You knew there were alternatives to what they said was socialism; there was insistence on what had been brought in, donated, and how you could lose it all. There could be a stepping back, a retroceding, a dead-end: another realm, sterility. Now, you know. *This* is the alternative: where we are now. It's what was foretold. You must see, that where we are, there's no alternative to the alternative we have, have reached. It would be illogical.

'It's sombre, not dark nor light, not eerie and not bright. The half-light's often been described. It's what there is when there aren't walls, there's only space, and canned light, stirred in with the dark.'

'You're right,' he says, 'and – what difference does that make? And Alex – I'm a messenger, that's all. I'm told to tell you – don't ask your customers 'why did you come?' For you, it's philosophy – for them, an insult. For management – it's bankruptcy. The thirsty come not to be alone. To be drunk, and after – to be sober. To play footsie with a friend: an enemy: a stranger. There's no philosophy. I know you think "the meaning of the world must lie outside the world". The meaning of the beerhall ... maybe it's the same. It doesn't seem so, if you come, get drunk, get laid potentially, leave, get thrown out.... There's no room for speculation. Probably that's why they come. "Outside": what does that mean? Stars? Other people? Thinking or speaking? And what kind of meaning do you want, or recognise? That all is structured? Like a language, or that language is structured like an everything?'

'Usually they mean,' I say, intrigued by Sandy's grasp – 'There is a meaning but our part in it's so small we cannot understand. Or else – the meaning is too great, articulated … a plan of some immortal architects, too big to reveal itself to us, who're objects of it; not comprehending subjects....'

'Emily got this job for you,' says Sandy, looking alarmed and hoping no one else has heard: 'Suppose some authority looks back at what we thought, and forward to what we two might do.... Consider, Alex! Without Emily – we'd be prisoners here, and this a jail. Accept the paradox. We feel we're moderately free because the biggest criminal outside has made it so: a fix. Our freedom rests on us, obedient criminals, being protected by the network of the bigger boss. That's quite some good! Emily decides, of course. We might vote her in, and she'd be chief, and she'd decide that all of us – should be in jail.'

'Emily is small,' I say, thinking of tantalising nights, hugging her on divans and motorcycles – 'She'd be replaced by someone just the same, or nearly so. Don't personalise the world. That's got us into trouble many times....'

'That's not the point,' says Sandy. 'She does what must be done – in the space left by the laws. We are professionals – most people – they are amateurs. They defraud, wheedle, lie, hide wills, deceive their partners, evade ... Life for most, Alex, is fiddling and be fiddled. They make victims – we're on a bigger scale. Pain doesn't interest us, nor family, nor love nor broken hearts.

'People fear and despise the law – they don't study it. You rarely ask what laws there are when you do what you will. She does what we humans must – move stuff and people, take revenge, punish for what's done or not. The law – it changes with the times and interests: sometimes wants to change ideas, sometimes to undo the past. It depends on where you are, and under what regime. The law is unpredictable in what it does and what it says. Emily is all known quantities. Big crime is more rewarding work than the making of a little country where everyone's like you.'

'I know,' I say. 'You've got it right. She is dependable.'

Sandy is succinct. He sees what I struggle to understand.... I think of Silke, Dagmar and the rest, my origins, poor Jarrett – who all laid out a human path you didn't notice as you paced along, your eyes sun-blurred, or pinched against the dust you raised... until you find it's all familiar. Not only underfoot, but landscape, time of day, your tiredness, brain that flashes on and off.... It's repetition. It's a design, a pattern.... lights spaced out with dark.

'The path,' I say, dismayed, 'Sandy! The path – always the same, the journey that they rave about – ends always in the place it's ended many times before.'

'It's comforting,' he says. 'We're monkeys in a tree. Forget our funny noses, paddle-shaped, our massive leaps, our clan, our family. The first and last ripe fig for each tastes just the same, exactly like it did for gran.... Maybe the last before you die – is slightly tough and dry, but never mind ... That is your passage and your destiny. You've done precisely what you could and what there was for you to do. Enough! Be thankful you weren't eaten early, put in a zoo, or in the lab; or saved! Re-cast in human likeness! What a fate! More millennia, another day and other dollars ....'

*

'How shall I end up, Sandy, if I'm not eaten?' I ask him.

'Walking,' he says, 'but blind. What distance can you feel then? A metre? Best not even walk. Don't think of a seeing dog – a dog can't feel or smell for you, or tell you colours. You won't have companionship – you're querulous now, mean and suspicious, argumentative – you like to be seen as tolerant, but you're intolerant of any prejudice, anything that irritates, and that becomes a pain. Women? A woman? Women don't say, but they avoid. They tolerate, but all those they dislike – they shun. It's worse than bigotry. She'll keep away from you.

'Men? You should have gone for gay: now, it's too late. You sag like an octopus. You resent youth – it left you, left you a squashed pumpkin; you'll never hook a Ganymede.'

'My turn,' I say – 'Your fortune, Sandy....'

'No, no,' he says. 'No games. No revenge, I don't need puffing up or taking down. I tell the truth in drips and drops – when it suits. I don't get off on seeming bright. I'm gold, don't tarnish, don't depreciate. Am sought, and always current and desired.'

'We both belong to Emily,' I say. 'Our future's in her memory.'

'Oh,' Sandy says, 'she wouldn't tell on us. She's a system: we're bugs and butterflies, her world, we flutter-burrow round. We're a swarm of evil fairies – you'd not catch many with a swat.... Besides – we're her creations.'

'Since you raised it, Sandy, I can go further about meaning,' I say. 'Meaning's not inherent, it's imposed. It comes from outside – I, and you – we're the outside. It means – that anything has meaning: if we determine that it does. We draw a meaning out, we make it manifest.'

'You follow Emily,' says Sandy. 'She's a dictator too. So – what did the steppe mean to you?'

'That I was poor at breaking horses, Sandy. And,' I say, 'the horses knew. So did they all, my friends. Especially those who knew the whole, or larger parts of it. How it all worked – not just falling in the grass, breaking a leg.... The sales. The horses knew they would be sold. They might run away, but not escape: anyone who saw them knew – they were broken, broken animals....'

'You mustn't flinch, Alex,' says Sandy, exasperated. 'Do what you always do. Accept. Don't wring your hands.'

'My friends,' I go on, 'had other trades. Sales, and traffics. They set the price, and paid the costs.'

'Like us,' he says, 'if you don't stake your life, you never get a shot at immortality. Put everything you have on some number that appeals, and get the buzz. Make a fortune, bet it all. Then see what someone gives you for yourself.'

*

Carrying the steins is tough. So's speaking Czech.

The project – Emily's – is simple. There's budgets, with conditions. Twirl them round and round – and in the end there's nothing spent, all notarised and out of time – and all the cash is yours. You need to buy some greedy guys along the way – but Sandy and I, we're playing with our lives. Freedom and reputation – we have none, we don't get *fiches* for those. Cash – is not a goal, it's compensation.

My problem's still – my dead friend, and my friend the executioner....

'Dementia's in your blood, Alex,' Sandy says. 'Your father was an artist in that line ... with all those beauties, wating for a slice of him – a slice as fine as those old Soviet brains were cut, to see how genius materialised. Who to try? Gorky? Lysenko? Not so many politicians.

Not Stalin, I would guess. Now, brain butchering – there's a job that calls! Simmered with an onion, a *lacrimosa* for my choice....'

That generation, my father's – they were sick, all got infected. We're healthy – that's for sure … cured.

'Jarrett was victim of imagination,' I put in: 'Alas, we all have one, maybe a miniature – but there's no link between them all, nor any two! Sex, money, all that stuff – we recognize: and bond with people who attract. But my imagination doesn't speak to yours, nor yours to mine. It's our safe, our refuge – a submarine for one....'

'You're a great guy, Alex,' Sandy says, 'You know nothing. Talking to you is filling up a well – then, a release, like peeing in the sea. But – you are timid. We must gull these official types, suck them in, compromise them, corrupt and threaten them.

'Take penguins. Here, guys see them on the screen, they're cute. They're useless. No hands – they're clumsy with their feet. Already they're abandoned in the icy parts, but people here would love to see them put on rafts, re-located in the Baltic sea. That way, there'd always be a docu movie scene! And so much cash and benefits! Penguins don't spend. *We* cost, Alix. Get busy with the guys who come in here.... They have expenses....'

'I thought,' I say. 'The birds, if they are such, they'd have to stay down south....'

'Everyone must learn to move,' he says. 'We're in act five, dénouement … in the melt, the climax, global climacteric; heating up. Catharsis is imminent. Penguins! We'll never visit them, but they're eternal stars. The cinema! will keep them living when reality is dead. Start small, Alex; a tiny sweetener is offered to re-settle, coddle them. It can be ours! Set to!'

'No, no,' I say. 'Potemkin icebergs? No fakery, Sandy! I come from tragedy: this is farce.'

'No,' he says. 'It's a test. Of you. Penguins: or back to horses. Prove yourself.'

'They have a holy book,' I say. 'It starts off – "I am writing a history of the Penguins." Penguin Island? If you succeed, the saga will become more sombre, the creatures more hemmed round.... Even, in a way, abandonment can seem an exploitation. Robbery....'

'That's been your choice,' says Sandy. 'You're on the side of bad. You specialised in the good sides of the bad, and overlooked the overdose, the slavery....'

'It's not quite so,' I say. 'Anything you do – design a car, a plane, a bomb. A *farmakon*. A savings plan. You dwell on the angelic side.... Those roasted corpses, weeping adolescents – you ignore. Better by far to knap your flints in peace, and not eat meat, or fight a tribal war! In the good, there's bad and vice versa, dialectically.'

'Don't look for meaning,' Sandy says, laughing. 'It's like fishing – nothing: or more than you can eat. And don't load everything on to intention. Don't say you intend, mean, well: it doesn't work that way. You "intend" to make a million and die in bed. Good for you. It doesn't dent reality, and if you had a soul, it would wear thin at the words....

'Salvation? Redemption? Already, it's too late.'

'Virtue may end well,' I say, 'though I am sceptical. Crime – has no good end.'

'You're tall to be a jockey,' Sandy says. 'Rodeos, perhaps, but it's hard, harder than the gallops, and the jumps, and you are skinny. You'll fall and break. The trouble is, you're one of the species that descends directly from the father. There is no rethinking: – you started bad, without a fashion or a character – wrong colour, sex – and if you're not a boss, it's because you're stupid, can't see how. Nothing you might change is credible: dull evil, that's the stereotype. Dull good – no one will care.'

'And you, Sandy?' I ask him.

'A Hussite,' he says. 'It's made for me. No one questions patriots – those can think exactly what they like.'

'People have big ideas,' I say. 'They're never realised. That's how you can corrupt – anyone. The best is easiest – there's more frustration, more bigness in their heads, and these naive guys – you buy them with a promise ... to stand beside the ones they once made to themselves.'

'Nature can't be bought,' says Sandy. 'And can't be saved. The cash is given, to save face, but it's far too late. Pigs or penguins. Going, going … rare: extinct. The money belongs to us – us guys who didn't cause disaster, didn't do anything, really. We didn't help, we didn't destroy – now, we'll take what's left, and run. Only kangaroos have wallets, purses, and there's none here – the other creatures, they can't carry cash or cards....'

'You mean,' I say. 'Jump ship? Steal from Emily? You and me?'

'It's easy,' Sandy says. 'Jumping ship in landlocked countries – you don't wet your feet. Me – I'm off to Slovakia ... a hidden place, full of people hiding, no one looks for them. You must go elsewhere, Alex. I'll give you what you need to get away. The rest is mine. You're soft, I run no risk in telling you.... You're a moralist, a sinner – your type's happier with smallish gain.'

'You say Slovaks are always pleased to see anyone,' I say. 'You could bring little gifts.... Here!' And I give him handfuls of matches, with blue heads. 'Hand them out – guys smoke – it's novelty....'

'They say deserters give these out,' says Sandy. 'Who knows why.'

He's dressed in drag, a coppery wig – he's very tall, looks like he's been in burlesque shows – 'My passport,' Sandy says, adapting his voice, 'Says I'm woman. I told them at the embassy: they said it was a joke.'

I'm curious. 'I may not need to show,' he says, 'but if I go further on.... And, Alex, I recognise those matches – you get them when you are in jail....'

'It was Le Havre,' I say. 'It was a mistake, another joke. My passport. Some other guy's, I guess. I don't smoke, but you can still set fires with them....' I want to be rid of them: 'Jail?' I say. 'I told you – a mistake. They let you out if you can't stand it.'

Sandy's impressed. 'That, I hadn't heard. It's very good to know.'

'Don't give me money, Sandy,' I say. 'It looks like payment for the matches. Those are a mistake.'

'All right,' he says. 'A Slovak welcome awaits me anyway,' and he raises his tall wig, a salute.

I say, 'An insult – to womanhood.' We laugh.

If Emily finds he's robbed her, I must be clean; not take Sandy's stolen money.

*

'The matches,' Emily says. 'They were a giveaway. They thought he had escaped from pokey. He won't escape from me!'

'He's held, then?' I ask. 'They fired me. Now, there's waitresses. And the cellar's full of cops. The women are as ripe as sharks – beautifully turned – to go between the tables, flicking a tail, and the broad mouths, always a smile. I feel like Neruda ... supple, granitic, spied upon....'

'No!' Emily shouts. 'You are not worthy. Robber of nests! And of me! Not a mention of Neruda, my inspiration, my traduced twin, my untouched destiny, not attained, not yet at least....'

I forgot – her writing ... her debts, her imitations, models – the colours, the tastes – much sharper, more accessible, than Neruda's country; than any country.

'Neruda here, now,' I say. 'Is just a gewgaw, a circle of bright stones. The people here – they spit upon his politics.'

'It was not to be,' she says. 'And you must not desecrate. Is there love here? No. There's beer. Cash sequestered from the guys who earned it, given to the penguins. It was up to Sandy – but greed got him, Alex. Treachery, and egoism. His family – they were travellers, and he – he took the dark path.'

'He's in jail?' I ask.

'I am his surety,' she says. 'He's mine. He owes me, every way. I am his law.'

'He's free?' I ask. 'I don't begrudge him that.'

'Arise!' she says. 'My champion, and my knight! Do you begrudge anybody? 'Arise, ye prisoners of starvation, ye wretched of the earth'. Sandy forgot. Maybe no one will rise again, not ever. They were – they are – not up to it. The message has been out for years. It could not be done. It's dead, and we're the carrion-eaters, the vultures, picking over the dead, the moribund ... cajoling, ransoming, anticipating, pandering. Taking our cut. Corrupting the weak, tripping up the strong. Giving the multitudes what they want – the people who couldn't manage it, the arising, the waking of the human race! Freedom: described exactly in the books and on the walls. Too bad. It became a bore, it fractured into trivia. We have to live, meanwhile. It didn't happen, Alex, the uprising. They tired, they were betrayed – what did they expect, when they had failed? Being fucked by mountebanks! That's what. We came along, and we're sweeping up the breakages. Picking over rubbish, mountains of it, re-sales, re-cycles.'

'I hadn't thought that way,' I say.

'My vengeance,' she says, 'is not secondary, not a passing mood. Not for the loss – for the disobedience. Sandy's.'

'We pledged, Emily,' I say: 'Us, to ourselves; not to profit.'

She gestures, shakes me off, dismisses my loyalty. What does my loyalty do for her? It's only mine, and irksome too.

'In the long run,' she says. 'All hopes are disappointed – in short runs too. But I don't let that influence me. If you want life – I give you life. If you want death – that too.

'The choice is yours, not mine, I don't advise. Life and death both cost – everything costs, but in the long run, there is only life and death. I take your fare, whichever shore you want to be dropped off on. I charge a tariff, and I don't seek wealth. It accumulates; but expenses, they do too.'

'What should happen, Emily?' I ask. 'That would upset your accounting, the book keeping, make you think – "Haha! I'm something special, I've done something remarkable, and they've noticed me...." An honour? Prize? A critique?'

'Silly boy,' she says. 'Don't wheedle me. Think of your Jarrett, eaten by those hyenas, those women he had trusted.... Sucked empty by his story-spinning Jenny. Perfidy, Alex. Watch out for it – it's the mark of our equality. Everyone is vulnerable, open to betrayal.

'I told you – I sell life and death. There's nothing more. And you are called to play your little part.'

There's a long pause. I wonder – how will it end?

She says, 'I got Sandy moved to a women's prison. A mistake! How shall we turn it? How will he pay his debts? How would Kovan pay his debt to Horab – Kovan killed him once: you can't do more than that to anyone. Nothing you do will change the sum.... Death annuls all debts. Be satisfied – accounts were settled, don't take out another loan. No debit and no credit – that's the way, the clean way, you should go.'

'Then Sandy,' I say. 'He owes.'

'Oh yes,' says Emily: 'He knows how to run. It's not where you end up; that is flexible – it's where you start your flight from. Hmmm. Slovakia. Yes – that was quite masterly.'

'My father, who you know about,' I say. 'I told you, when we were cold writers, thinking of a story we could live: – he hallucinated, but he didn't need to buy a cure.

No drugs, just the genius he had. I think I am the same – I make my own potions, my own free fall, free flight....'

'Oh yes,' says Emily, and laughs. 'My writing. It's because I can do anything – I wanted to show how good I was at that. You are unlucky, Alex – you invent, I imitate. You imitate, of course, but you have the shapes inside, and as they change, so, you are confused. Your universe explodes, chairs walk, your snakes climb ladders to the roof. I plan, so everything is ready for the off.... But you're unfortunate. You rely on your imagination; like I said, no one can share it. You're a dud. And as for hallucinations – normal people trek on like soldiers: they take the pleasure when they can, and the longing for a death, theirs or another's – it drives them on. They work, they march, they dig, they run – little soldiers: forward and back; for them it's like the factory, delivering stuff, digging a ditch, or herding sheep.

'They look backwards – keep accounts: children procreated, millions made, and lost, a pension maybe, men and women – screwed or not ... They die, loaded with time remembered, regained or lost, encrusted with their doings like a venerable oyster's shell.

'You – look forward. The past – is empty. Don't buy the pills, the smoke, a waste all that: – your life is always yet to come. It's future: a lived hallucination! Your problem is, my dear, you've no death wish, and even killing wouldn't register. The normal ones – they balance life and death – not you....'

She would go on with her guess. I interrupt: 'And you, Emily. What are you?'

'I let the people do exactly what they want,' she says. 'I told you. Choose life, or death. I'm quite indifferent.'

'Not what I asked,' I say. 'What are you, Emily?'

It's not any easy question. There's no satisfactory answer, though all answers are correct, including 'I don't know'. But some are an evasion....

'Don't forget,' she says, 'I am your boss, you don't exist except to do my will. And if you don't – that's not significant. I'll find another you, at once.'

'You're a spider, Emily,' I think, careful not to say so – 'You package us, your shit-eaters: hang us from your ceiling....'

'I once felt,' she says, 'you were a plague. Now I see – it's evolution. From bacteria comes the plague and all the saints.'

'That's not it at all,' I say. 'It's business. If not by you, it's me or anyone that runs it. Bosses usually are warriors, or crazy. You are a mystery in full sight because you have satisfactions none of us can grasp.'

'Everyone has those,' she says.

'It isn't that at all,' I say, or maybe – I just think. I'm a fantasist, but Emily's a liberal. She's not responsible for anything – though everybody else is. She does nothing bad or good. And yet – badness swirls around her. It must be attractive. It is to me, although I'd rather be a victim than a perpetrator. My view is – if you don't will good – which makes you intolerable – you must will bad. We bring it on ourselves, of course, but even so – we like to see it, shove it along, it isn't pleasure, isn't *Schadenfreud.* It's wanting to see bad go on, increase. It's a proof, I don't know how I should react to 'good'. It's why I'm attracted to Emily. My friend is killed – so, was it bad? Was he? I've no idea. I'd like to do some bad myself, just to redress, bring justice. How can I know? Friends do bad things to friends, and good things too – all at the same time.

Sandy doesn't end up well in jail. His mistakes – they come to seem insulting; vengeance comes, over and over, very slow and sure.

'What will suit you, Alex?' Emily seems to ponder ... doing an assessment, like Immigration or a bank: 'Corruption? – not even E for Effort, I'm afraid. Hallucinations – you already have them. Putting you in sales is useless; then there's chance and tarts, intimidation and protection, public contracts and our debt collection. Advancing credit, letting people in and out, supervising law and bureaucrats, arms, aviation – almost everything is our concern. We do it better than the state, and have no debt, no public scandals, and the boss is always right – and if it isn't so, they're not the boss....' We laugh.

'I'm distraught,' I say. 'I've no vocation, obviously. Most people manage. They're carers, managers and cops ... landlords and dealers, barmen and barflies ... Moreover, they have partners, dogs and cats, favourite movies....'

'You could form opinions,' Emily says. 'That's all that's left. Change taste and sensibilities – but I don't want that stuff contracted out. That hilly province – is all mine....'

I don't weep. I might.

'Here,' says Emily, brightening up. 'My grannie's recipe. The *Beruf* stone,' and she puts a brown stone with a crude hole in it tight against my eye. 'The calling. The best banks use this,' she says, 'to recruit.'

There is mist. Honestly, I see nothing: maybe the stone itself. 'And was your grannie Slovak?' I ask her.

'Oh no!' says Emily.... 'From the Banat. The answer's there – exactly where you saw. In mountains: the Carpathians, maybe the Rockies. Atlas. You're a guide. You will lead the starving and the wretched, guide them where, or nearly where, they want to go. People must move, the reason's always sound. We all came out of Africa, you know – it took us years, because, of course, there was no guide. That is your calling, Alex....'

And she improvises on.

'Usually, it's locals, Emily,' I say, 'that navigate.'

*

I am dismayed. Wandering near the frontiers, dodging the cops, surveyed by drones.... No!

The steppe calls. That is home.... Frontiers? Deserts used to be ideal, they swallowed armies, that way it was said they could bring peace. But down came the Hyksos, out of somewhere.... Barbarians on the steppe, swimming rivers, crossing seas in bone coracles, making causeways of their dead, crossing over. Acquiring new gods and architecture.

Everybody crosses over – personally, or making someone else a bridge.

Learning our languages: 'how much', 'when', 'no', 'tomorrow', 'sleep'.

If you don't have a desert, then mountains will do – 'yahbooing' to your lookalikes over the ridge. Oesho, god of high windy places – everybody venerates Him....

'All right, Emily, I'll try,' I say.

'I knew you would,' she says.

Sandy ends real bad – in pieces, like Orpheus, though Sandy couldn't hold a note, went looking for no one but himself. His head – silent; the tongue twisted. Someone steals the wig.

MOUNTAINS

Mountains. They're not rugged, spiky, not like the Alps. Don't dare you to climb them. Supine, like immense stone pregnancies, over and over – without snow, or animals, no grey, no ice. Brown dusty humps – Afghans trying to go to Turkey, Iranians to Pakistan. I am a solitary angel, waiting for my fugitives, penitents, sinners, anyone: desperate and hopeful.

Any movement up here is of concern to me. There's no signal – there would be just a line of people, resentful of past and future, silent and frightened, suspicious of me, as they should be. I'm not benificent – I'm the stone in the spate, the single stone you must jump from the shore to hit and stick to.... No one, not me either, knows if I'm anchored, if I'll hold, or maybe I'm insubstantial, a piece of discard, a paper bag, a sign 'Danger!', a plastic shape snagged in the white water....

But there's no water here. Shale, brown crumble, sharp green pebbles – a mineral, low value, the lode stripped off long since – miners, scavengers, their baskets full of rocks bending them double ... running like apes – long gone.

I'll have come out of Africa: then for many lifetimes into the black, the cave shared with bats and bears.

I'll have found a compromise here – mountains with no caverns, without shelter and security, under the scalding sun. Something neither cave nor desert, and I'll have acquired a psychology – a dream of forests: a mind – lianas, snakes. Butterflies and vampires. Fear, the first, most enduring, of emotions: and anxiety. Is there ever safety, security, a person? No persons here. I've lost all that, in my heart, those two emotions, the twins, fear and anxiety.

No mind: just staring, wondering if that patch that seems to move is people: clients, fugitives, waiting to be taken down, and on, a history lesson, where we don't exchange a word. They throw away a culture like a bag too heavy; then, unencumbered, think a new climate awaits; perhaps.

Angels are lonely, and you seldom spot them. Emily may have seen me not as guide, but guardian: a Zoroastrian figure, staring at her across the unquenchable fire – without a thought or temperament.

Angels protect, inspire: they don't guide. Guardians don't lead. No one will run after you – I can escape from everyone. Emily won't care that I've jumped ship, That I can't swim on land. Ridiculous!

I fear, so I defend. Charon guides. Circe lures. Those two know where they're taking you – I've no idea. If I had clients, I'd know where their next stage begins, but as to destination.... No idea. I accompany, I'm the life and death – their representative, the commercial fellow-traveller that Emily identified. I'm nothing: a stretch of road, of time ... a ghost who takes them from their old ghosts to the new.

The refugees would be too tired and tense to notice me.... We're a piece of time with figures. And the wind – its grand indifference ... to chimes, to soughing in the trees, to prayer-flags – to the mountain god who sits on top of every top: the wind, it doesn't care for that, for them, for Him, and as for twanging on a roof, rattling a window, huffing down a tile, it's not its business, not at all, it's there to blow unfettered – around and up and down the mountains, all the better if there's nothing there to make a noise. Not there to be breathed, to have you open arms to it, or button up, lash down, or turn your back on it. Wind! Is there to blow, no purpose, no direction, for ever, on and on.

And still no people. and it's good, it's excellent, I can lie lumpish in my stone age, invent my legs, run, grow fancies, horrors, invent divinity, invent theology, invent a heaven and climb into it, wear bedsocks, make a sword, give it an edge, take and put my neighbour's head in a round case, carry it on my shoulder like a telephoto lens, invent electricity, and space and time, climb into them and disappear ... and find myself waking, alone up here, knowing everything, not speaking, a perfect specimen, the last, the first.

When there is nothing left, there will be the wind, there will always be the wind until there really is nothing left at all.

I'm innocent. Grubby, perhaps: denying that the scum on my skin is mine. It comes from the necessities, environment, the struggle for survival. Don't believe me, don't believe what my documents might say, nor what I say my story is. It's a mistake, a clerical error, someone else's statements, a dossier that doesn't take me into its account. The dead and pending – they are not included – that's the law, protecting you, protecting you from law. My statements – you tell them to the cops, the boss. Believe them – what you can, or less.

*

'There was no one, Emily,' I say. 'I walked all over. Tried every mountain. No people. Nothing.'

'That was the effect I wanted, Alex,' Emily says. 'No one, not even you. You roamed and thought. When someone thinks, there is a void, you know,' she says. 'Thinking is like that. The scenery recedes, an empty stage is not a stage. No one. Absence. It's a good lesson. How can thinking lead to anywhere, when there is nothing there? That's what you must understand.'

'You're right, of course,' I say. 'It's not original. When we think, 'we' are not present, no one is – or maybe ... it's an activity that joins us up, somehow, like whales, making sounds ... an ocean away the song is batted back.... Except, with us: you think ... and there's no song, no echo, no response....'

'Forget the whales, Alex,' Emily says. 'I hoped you'd find a reason for what you do in what I do....

'Sandy: going to Slovakia – a girl acquired, no doubt, his bride, in braids, a baby somewhere, horse-cart to the church, if that is their belief.... And then – comeuppance, the dreadful fate. All of us – we each have one of those in waiting: a fate. Maybe several.

'You were a conduit, Alex, up in the mountains without snow or ice – all that was required was to find the needy people, pass them on.You did not find, you were not found. You thought, that's all. Who are you, what's the meaning of what you do, what happens when you fail ... you didn't think of that – you thought of emptiness, of mountains mute and purposeless....'

'Yes,' I say. 'it's history. Everbody dies, is hung upon their deadwood tree, on a trunk that grows, but has no leaves, no heart, no sap, no green ... a totem. Name and number graven. A spread of inky branches. They've become ancestors, yoked to their forebears, siblings, offspring, like spans of oxen....'

'No,' she says. 'Forget duration. Why did no one come, up there, in the heights? Do you think everyone was satisfied, decided to stay where they had found themselves?'

I laugh. 'Of course,' I say. 'I may have been in the wrong place. The armies and the cops – may have found our routes. Repression, betrayal ... an interruption. That would explain....'

'Exactly,' Emily says. 'And after all your thinking, you're not being there, nor anywhere, but in your inexplicable, incommunicable activity – the Thought! – was there an answer, a resolution to what I'm asking you? Where were the people that you didn't see? Happy? In jail? Pursued and hunted down...?'

'Oh,' I say, irritated by her simplicities. 'I'm sure everything was going on just like before. Not there alone, but everywhere. They needed me, and alas, we did not meet. The same as everything we do, the need is there.... Hands reach out, hands do not join...'

We leave it so, with neither satisfied.

*

I re-live the life I miss more often than I live the one I have. Silke, Dagmar, and the despoliation of poor Jarrett.... I couldn't bear existing in that way – ageing, sickness, accommodation for an other, others ... a dislocated limb snapped back into a socket, you feel it always, being normal, back in place – it's never right, never the true alignment, something has truly snapped.

'You could do publicity,' says Emily. 'Tell people, "on the whole, I'm good". You can invest in me, I'm a sure thing.'

'It's to be considered, Emily,' I say.

I'd sooner get out from under her. Start my own scheme. Become autonomous. Load my dead friend and his killer on my back, Zorab and Kovan, making up my life – the burden of the dead, the living; life is the murderer.

Taking to my road, being very careful not to drop anyone. You must make excuses, or bear guilt. Neither are due, neither are yours. Already, it's heavy, the weight of those two – and then there's Sandy.... Just take on his head, already you are staggering....

'Publicity,' says Emily, 'seeking the good, and spouting it out, a fountain primed with wine – runs now with red, and now with water. That – or chance. You could try cards. Fix craps. Have a table, weight the wheel – a wrinkle in the carpet will tilt luck your way.'

'I know how everything works,' I say. 'I know how you exploit a place, its people, and how there's others try to turn it round, bring cash until there's something stops it – a river dries, the trees catch pox....'

She laughs. 'You could go work in a poor country and do some deals – until they chase you off, you bring prosperity. If you're not greedy, people will remember you, put asters on your tomb.'

'I've thought of that,' I say. 'I'd need a bigger personality.'

'Someone might sell you theirs,' she says. 'They're an encumbrance, personalities. I keep mine with the bicarb and the senna pods.'

We laugh. I touch Emily's ear: usually she shoos me off. 'Most beautiful women don't have lobes,' I say. 'Yours are like grapes. Little plums, in the making. There are Italian plums called "nuns' thighs" – sweet, shaped like emerald drops....'

'Enough, Alex,' she says, pulling away, my hand still clutching. It must have hurt her ... 'You writers are cruel bastards. Sentimental and hypocritical. Failed writers – like you: even worse. Those poor horses! One in five makes it to market, the rest are discards. All around you they die, are mutilated, animals and humans – but on you go, smiling, preening.... I don't want you around. Do the count, if you're unsure, your mates do really really bad: you're poison, dear.'

'It isn't how it looks to me,' I say.

'You straight guys,' she goes on. 'Bend your women like they're Parthian bows. That's how we're bottom heavy. Your self-deprecation, your pretend-retreat –

then off you fire your arrows...! Anyway, remember what happened to the Parthians....'

'I know,' I say. 'Some are Kurds now. There is my problem....'

'You don't have problems,' Emily says. 'You have devastating solutions. Your mad father – abandoned. Poor Sandy – seeking love, losing his head....'

'The pain of the world, Emily,' I tell her. 'You must know, it's what we live ... *Weltschmerz.'*

'No,' she says. 'You seek people in dramatic circumstances – the barrels over Niagara Falls. Decisive outcomes – other people have them, you record them. You direct – you never act. If there is no cliffhanging – you procure it. Anything will do: pink or white marshmallow? Play the preference. It's what you call your universe: really, a patch the same size as your feet. Choice without significance....'

*

In my dream, someone is telling me, 'If you can't do it, don't insist. Give it up, or else your life will pass through the gates and go into an unknown landscape.'

'I work with horses,' I say. 'So no landscape is unknown. This must be Turfan, there must be a king, and maybe further down, by the river, there's a kind of state, a federation – what do they want with kings? It's desert. Coinage, perhaps, imitating, choosing a language and a script, a tamga.... There'll be a river – for the horses. The Amu-Darya? Otherwise – it's camels.'

All this is plausible. I finish off the liquor – *raki* – and remember I'm without work. Maybe – take a step down, in the kitchen. In the shade of the kebab mountain. Get taken on, plan. Join some guys – not a gang, Turks won't trust me, but just for once, and enacting my idea, if only I could have one....

'Emily gives people what they want,' I say. 'She's a big boss, of crime, desire, necessity. She gives them life, death: or mobility. The clients – they want peace or death. That's antiquity. The present avoids mentioning both those, though it brings death in loads. The law, modernity, science – gives people what they do not want, but what there is, set up from the beginning, waiting for humanity to suffer for predestination. Rules, restraint, an explanation of the universe.'

I go on. There's no one there, no one to listen: I am asleep: 'Modern life is curiosity. Not of the drastic kind, not peeking, pulling it all down ... science tells you "everything is knowable". All becomes a commonplace – so, curiosity is appeased, contained, routine.'

MEHMET

I need an interlocutor – I'm still feverish, reinfected, maybe moribund. Is this still the dream, the freezing night with Emily? It's thirsty work, this being sick, infected … a desert. Mehmet the barman – carrying saddles, pouring hooch … I need someone to help me mount the camel, and to tell him where I'm bound. Point me, spur us on – it's quite clear where I want to go, I think.

I'm quite drunk, I'd say. 'It's a challenge we can face, you and I, Mehmet: not to take either path, but choose another, absolutely independently....'

'That's not it,' says Mehmet. 'Not it at all. It's reactionary, your idea; leads by the nose. And – it leaves no space for us. Emily – I'd guess she respects the ancient code, the law of feuds and rustling cows. It means not life, nor death – it's a perpetual enslavement. The feud, the *faida* – it has no end, it loses purpose, forgets its beginning. It's families, it's stasis, Alex, nobbling pigs and roasting them; and potshots from the thicket.

'Emily – sells you what you need, not what you want. Modernity can't do that, and science isn't interested. Hers is a market for selling stolen goods.'

'She's a cannibal?' I ask. 'Honour among thieves, blackmailer's code, it's venerable, it's artistry. Is science indifferent to difference? There's same and different – no preference.

'Science – the laws, the manifestations – is always there, but if you don't seek it – it doesn't care. It's the ten centavos coin that rolls beneath your chair, looking exactly like your own ten cents, but valid only in Brazil.... It fits in everywhere, in every slot. Value is something else. The coin fits, it is not counterfeit. That should be enough.'

I'm losing the idea ... away it goes. Ten centavos – enough to pay to get me where I'd want to be, among the horses...?

'You're drifting, Alex,' Mehmet says. 'Much of Brazil is steppe, or steamy taiga. Science and ten cents won't help you there – leave it! Find, don't copy.'

'Make, don't find,' I say.

We neither of us have much of an idea. Maybe Emily is not a contrast, not to anything, just a part of what there is, a bug upon a leaf, an aphid on broad leaves, without a fruit. Making do, improvising, uncaring....

'What is science to you, Mehmet?' I ask him.

'It's nothing,' Mahmet says. 'There's no such thing. It shows you there is nothing but what's there. That is the start.'

'It's where we've been. The cycle starting once again,' I say. 'We shall discover every fantasy and myth, and at the end find science that will sweep it all away: and there's the beginning once again, the myth. The cycle starts and so do we ... over and over. Those deserts of chalcedony, covered in codes and algorithms, the distances to far-off stars ... all calculated, then all forgotten: the savants eaten, turned into bone-meal for hungry skeletons.... Always the threat is there – keep it at bay with magic, then with science. Science – mixed in with magic. Both are cruel: the magic and its science.'

'There's interesting points and dead ends here, Alex,' Mehmet says. 'And of course, it's good to pass the time with you. The camel's empty – maybe she needs a drink. This bar is dead, I'd leave, but everywhere is slow – and I had hoped to find some deal with you. A little bent, perhaps, but not exactly dangerous....'

'Derring-do?' I ask. 'I outgrew it, but it's good to see it lingers.'

'My girl is tough,' says Mehmet. 'Tougher than me – she practises. Throwing people, hitting targets. Nesrine Nelyubov – to win her, I had to shovel anthracite. A metaphor – reality was harder still....'

'Courtship's not like interviews,' I say. 'Not like asking to work for the post office.'

'Well, here she is,' says Mehmet, making her appear.

'And what have you done all day?' I ask.

'Trying on frocks, like normal people,' Nesrine says. She's off an old-time movie set. Camera-ready, always. I don't stereotype, of course, or fetishise, but she is special, unique, perhaps. Out of my range, and Mehmet's too, I'd say. 'I hate normality,' she says. 'Those frock shops! I am perfect. They don't cater for me – clothes for monsters only, big and small....'

'I don't recognise perfection,' I say. 'Uniqueness? Certainly.'

'She cuts paths,' says Mehmet, holding her. She pulls away.

'And you, Alex – a Napoleon of crime?' she asks. We laugh.

'Chances come along,' I say. 'Though, the fates don't give out info, good luck is not a judge. Welcome aboard, Nesrine – there is no ship. But – there's an enormous sea.'

*

Mehmet chants – 'Unloved Nesrine, so sharp and clean….'

'Don't you love her, Mehmet?' I ask. It's like a scene from Simenon. Not much subtlety ... motives plain as flying buttresses.

'I do,' he says. 'It's her that doesn't love. Don't think of trying her.'

'In this job,' I press on, 'working the bar. You must meet many perfect people.'

'There's guys like you, with propositions,' Mehmet says. 'Horses mostly. Boxers. Loans. You're the only honest one, of course. The women and the men who're on the game, the amateurs, the chancers – they're mostly perfect. You need to be. But Nesrine's different – she enjoys being the clean one where others have no choice. Maybe she's a virgin – certainly she's avoiding martyrdom.'

'I'm not into that,' I say. 'Buying and selling. Sex and coups – no one gets rich, everyone gets coarse – this life, Mehmet, is a slime-pit. You may do well, but you can't climb out. The more you try, the dirtier you get.'

He's been pouring for other people, hasn't heard. 'You've a quaint way of expressing, Mehmet,' I say, 'Nesrine too. As if you've just learned English from a very old secluded person – their attitudes as well. "On the game". I've not heard that for years!'

'Nesrine does what she feels is good. What's right – it doesn't bother her,' he says. 'She's consistent, Alex....'

'She's beautiful,' I say. 'Symmetrical and free of blobs and wens – but after some hours, it palls. A picture, may cost you millions, but in a day or so – it's furniture. Nesrine – for sure she has a price – a lover's estimate, or achieved at auction.... All things beautiful set the price for ugly things.'

'Forget your Marx,' says Mehmet, slapping my shoulder hard, and laughing gruff. 'What you are paid is what it takes to stop you doing what someone set over you won't like. That's how they calculate the wage. Forget capital, supply, demand – or other noble words: you're paid to stay on-side. The lowest paid – they're really docile. The feisty ones – carry off a sack of gold. It isn't like you think, Alex – the poor are not exploited, they're the crowd who don't give trouble. They complain, and it stops there. Everywhere the rich – aggressive, selfish – ruling roosts and chicken coops, get paid heaps … not for what they do, which is banal, but to keep them quiet, pre-empt rebellion.'

'It's true, Mehmet,' I say, surprised. 'It's what my granny said – and so, I thought it must be crap. But – now, the obvious is right, it seems.... The economy – is ransom. From wages to the uppity, to rickety things you do not want....'

'Not all you think is stupid,' Mehmet says. 'Where you're stuck, is at philosophy. Philosophy – the poor man's magic, and the pauper's science. It isn't worth a spit – it's bits of is and lots of ought. A guy unqualified like you – you think you sit and write it down. It isn't so. Magic – does not transform. Science – is not humane. It's quite dismissive of us. It doesn't care – for anything. But philosophy, my dear – is faces in the fire.'

*

'Nesrine,' I ask. 'Will she betray? Or spy?'

For sure, I've woken up!

'She's all too human, Alex,' Mehmet says. 'Like you and me. True crime – concerns making us the cash we are not owed. The rest is down to hardship, to necessity.

'What do we want for breaking rules? Are we driven by our needs? – or wanting lots lots more for doing less? Fleeing a massacre – you will break some laws.... The law – always says that it is "one", coherent, indivisible. It isn't so. Take us. We break the law because it stops us being rich....'

'I'm not so sure, Mehmet,' I say. 'It seems more complicated. My eye sees always horses: free, running in packs ... the grass is shoulder-high, the sun is gold and spiked, like it is on flags ... I'm tranquil, happy.

This is life, Mehmet, and I'm alone, and – maybe I don't die, get sick, get dumped or robbed....'

'Well,' Mehmet says. 'You're full of fantasy. Remember what I said – Nesrine is not your business. It is mine. Keep off! – you are a wastrel, but you circle round the world without a brake or check, with no restraint.... Beware the accidents you'll cause – bring them on yourself, no one will care. Involve the rest of us – beware!'

*

Nesrine says, 'I have contacts with the strong guys, trying to run weak places ... Maybe—'

I interrupt, 'Nesrine – the soldiers and the spies – they try to run these states – there's lots of cash, they run the industries, the food, and all the rest, and take a cut. You won't get in! They know quite well how to skim, and have their courtiers take what's left. Spies flock to other spies – it's knowing that your enemies are really friends, closer to you than your brothers....'

'Honour among thieves?' asks Nesrine. 'Yes, I know all that. We are not thieves like them. We're artists, we make up rules.... Then, we don't follow them. Why should we?'

She never lies. Her perfume – lotus and opium.... The caravans? – I know the fragrance – a rasp of camel there, and in Nesrine too.... 'Yes,' she says. 'I know the only stable in this place – they let you ride the camels to the hills.'

I'm addicted to Nesrine. She is me, my memory, my past, my wished-for future.

Time wasted, with Emily: is it worth searching for it?

Nesrine says, 'I've thought a lot about our destiny. Those states that's founded on ideas – maybe a religion, or a revolution ... a founder, spirit immortal, warrior.... Here's my conclusion: after a generation, that's all gone, exhausted. The purpose, destiny – is a routine that you try to skip. Then comes the reckoning – the sacrifice. You must accept hard times – you're not obedient, or faithful, so the gods feel lonely, or there are further stages in the evolution of your state you hadn't known about. So – faith and fervour are replaced with sacrifice. All your fault ... and now you pay. You are the sacrifice, you suffer for your ignorance.'

'Where do we two fit in, Nesrine?' I ask.

My mind is empty: lotus and opium – they will fill the space.

'It's best I do not tell,' she says. 'Do what I say. The rest may be clear in time.'

'That's quite ridiculous,' I say. 'We can't be a syndicate of crime if one of us is ignorant of where and what....'

'No, Alex,' Mehmet says. 'She's right. It's best that no one knows the whole. It's a defence, you see – no one can betray the rest....'

'It's casuistry, Mehmet,' I say.

There's nothing I can do. Nesrine! – anyone who's straight would follow her – or maybe if you're not, you'd follow anyway. Charisma. Not sex, or liking. She speaks with all the inspiration that founds the states and sects, a talking Book – where, in the past, she says, we all went wrong ... Mehmet's her rock, and I – her simple follower. Her fan.

*

This perfection. Nesrine – you know, perfection does nothing, not for anybody: not you, who are perfect, and all who contemplate you. That is, you are not you, but you are perfect.

To contemplate perfection – is that your difficulty, or mine? Are we both troubled, in different ways, by different necessities...? It's personal, of course, but not about us. Consider the disastrous things perfect people are led to do, and have done to them.... We who contemplate you – we're forced to recognise how you are way ahead of us. We're ordinary – terribly so. In the end, we have to smash you, to save you from your belief in your perfection, our wanting it for ourselves, our hating your certainty, your illusion that instead – it's us who have invented it.... You have a miracle, but it isn't you. Your secret, Nesrine – you tell it freely. Perfection lasts, turns into sacrifice, its disenchantment, its opposite, and yet – a metamorphosis that is itself the cycle.... It has to be. Your perfection, you can't cash it in. You, who pass from light to destruction, a punishment-salvation ... your condition's terrible. It is your sad end – but what will you have done to reach it, how many others destroyed along the way? How many species, how many lookalikes, less perfect – won't survive until you make your sacrifice, your immolation? Till the next time, till another perfect one develops – not perfect in themselves, of course, but in the idea they have, and have us share it....

It's not a sickness, it's how humans go, in crowds, in organisations, in beliefs. In couples and in millions. The worm that eats the rose's heart knows perfection, its dance, its shape and sound, more intimately than anyone....

'Be careful, Nesrine,' I say aloud, out of nowhere. 'I'm the worm.'

'Too late,' she says, and laughs. 'I already have my worm: Mehmet.'

'We must be animals,' I say. 'We are. Those are all perfect. No big deal. It's in the chime "eat – be eaten". That's the refrain – when it stops, there's calamity in sight: the rungs fall out the ladder – there's two sterile poles left, that's all.'

'Perfection's wrong,' says Nesrine. 'It's you who used the word. It's how things ought to be. Universal, ordinary, a wonder.'

'Contraband? Ferrying people from bad places – into sometimes worse, or usually just ordinary. Very hard,' I say. 'Nothing special. I may try it. Fishing for luck.'

'You should not have begun this chase, Alex,' Nesrine says. 'I was wrong to join you. You are not trustworthy – it runs in your genetics. Hallucinations. You look for the essence of things. Things are things – that is their essence – look no further. People around you lose patience. Some lose their lives. Avoid that!'

It's true. Living is a dangerous business, so is being with horses – a mule can kick you in the head and kill you.

'Mehmet has a picture in his room,' she says. 'He's not allowed that, but it's there. It's of where he comes from, the interdiction. No one else cares – he does. An Iranian wouldn't be ashamed of their body, they nurture it.'

'That picture,' Mehmet says, 'is "the shape of God". It's a white sack, like a man in the moon, flown there in a baggy suit, like a balloon.... Did you know, Alex, our breath is a gas? We could fly anywhere, if we had the right envelope to wear, like mongolfiers.'

Nesrine giggles, irresistible.

*

'All right,' I say. 'Work your scheme, tell me what I'm to do. No one to lose their life. The oath "do what is good for you"; and look no further.'

'Look, don't tell,' she adds. 'Don't smuggle animals,' she adds. 'They want like us – the incompatibles:

freedom and food. It's a vain search ... our birth-curse, Alex....'

'Tell me what I am to do,' I say. 'No accusations....'

'What you didn't do in Prague,' she says. 'Poor Sandy – you just let him go.... He was rash. Then there was Jarrett – you did not take care. He hallucinated – now, you're doing it....'

'Tell me, Nesrine,' I say, ashamed, exasperated.

'Corrupt some guys who know what they have too much of, or absolutely nothing,' Nesrine says: 'Sell on the info ... anticipate. Secrets today – tomorrow they are commonplace. We get in that gap, between the confidential and the massacre.... Between state secret and the rioting. Sell on, don't meddle, don't take sides. We're middlemen and women – using intelligence. That's all.'

'We're clean,' I say. 'We're thinkers, intellectuals.'

She smiles, and nods. I know it isn't so. 'Don't tell your friends, nor Emily,' Nesrine says.

*

'Thugs and spies,' Mehmet says. 'They've come in swarms. Finding things out – is all political. We don't have soldiers—'

'What's difficult is always guarded, Mehmet. Once,' I say. 'They used dragons – now it's more complicated ... and rough. Dragons cost, they have a temperament – spies and thugs come cheap and plentiful....'

*

It's a problem, a disaster. China is back, where it once was, the centre of the civilised world. Remember their attempted circumnavigation – those huge ships, could easily have gone round the earth, and colonised America – ceased: halted. Come back! Too far. Too much. The order was obeyed! They gave up, enjoyed their primacy.... But the thinkers – they just thought, just think. They're hermits, the guys who didn't make it to become bureaucrats. They seek tranquillity, in failure and regret, passing their time, life – marooned among the toilers in the fields, the soldiers on the labyrinth of walls, facing the barbarians, the world that isn't you, not truly barbarism, but movement, a boon and challenge, 'the invention of nomadic cavalry': horsemen, steppe agglomerations, fluidity: the flow.

A philosophy, a passing of time: cultivating submission? The theme, that thinking is inert, can't travel.

Capitalism – has only the one idea.

Science is indifferent to us – it's everything that *isn't* us, that doesn't interest us, in our intimacy, our puzzled delicacy, in our skulls and skin. Science is about what *is* – and not at all about us, or about me....

'I love ideas, Mehmet,' I say. 'Toss them around, see how they grow and melt like snow, or turn into their opposites, like caterpillars and the butterfly. I love to see them at the dawn – a cloud of mayflies, due to die at dusk, and then the sun goes down, out come gruff frogs, and gradually you droop and sleep while they croak on....'

'Not being serious,' he says. 'Won't save you. You're just more vulnerable. The hunters don't believe in butterflies: all sides, each hunt, wearing the green, the red, will see you as a renegade, a terrorist, a terroriser: an easy mark....

'Your time has passed, my friend; the age of speculation, of otiose and careless play, is gone. Ideas are bombs and bullets now. Me and Nesrine, we won't protect you. No one will shield you, unless you take their oath, salute their flag ... pledge your immortal soul....'

'I've done dreadful things, Mehmet,' I say. 'To other animals as well as all the human ones. I've skittered round, not left a mark on anyone. But – I've kept my spirit clean, away from all the noise and dirt....'

'We need a country behind us,' Nesrine says. 'Alex, you would be a hindrance in our search. Is it land or sea – China or the States? Big countries – you need that. Brazil is burning, Russia melts – China is wedded to the land, she moves out of her walls – but maybe she's too big for us? We're relatively small, forgettable, for them, and disobedient. The Yanks can be quite picayune, first they inspect, then they desert their friends; the Russians kill their exes ... a conundrum. Mexico is full of crooks....' and on she goes, around the globe – it seems there's no one wants to share their shadiness with similars....

'It's Goldilocks,' I say. 'You want a place that is just right, apparently virginal, that sleeps with every kind of bear, including juveniles.... Turkey, Iran – you're down to middling powers, they shoot on sight, but being partners ... maybe not ... Italy, now, there's the Mob, but they're already everywhere, like the Yakuza ... they recruit at will .... I agree, it isn't easy, finding space to do your business....'

They turn away, Mehmet, Nesrine. I know too little. Do I retire? Do philosophy, or nurture bees?

'It's not to make a special point, Mehmet,' I say. 'I realised I was in a doubtful gang when my friend killed my friend. With Sandy – everything was clear. I'd crossed the line, by all accounts – and I was doing bad. And now, it seems you've found another line, where those who make the rules of good and bad are also hiring people to do bad ... making wars, spying and subverting – not to test the rules, but going quite outside them....'

'Yes, yes, Alex,' says Mehmet, irritated. 'Put it like that, and you have found what everybody knows but doesn't waste their time to say. You still insist that there must be a secret plan, the human drive behind all this, a mystery.

'All anyone can find that way is danger, threat, and cash. Vendetta, exploitation.'

'I don't think that's it, Mehmet,' I say. 'That's hindsight.'

'Maybe so,' he says.

I don't want goodness, I want to join humanity, and then go where I want to be.

COMPLICITY

'People wanting to be good,' I tell Nesrine. 'Make compromises. Accept the bad to avoid the worse. Accept collateral damage as a fact of nature, or of chance. Perfection, like innocence – where does that go, if it has ever been? It's dulled and grey. Like it or not, we say we seek the good, hoping the aspiration cancels out the bad ... "Good" in one sphere, "bad" regarding others. Manicheism. It leads you to accommodate ... Tolerant of intolerance. Survival – taken as a good self-evident.... Long long times to wait and contemplate....'

'It has to be,' says Nesrine. 'Otherwise there's neither good or bad.'

'To be human, we must accept the bad,' I say. 'And concentrate on doing bad; and see – where does that lead?

'Do, and take the consequence. The point is clear – defining good is not enough, it must be practicable. So, with the bad as well ... it's your weapon, see how it works against the good....'

‘Suppose you don’t find out?’ she asks. ‘Not ever. Don’t you see – there’s trains and trucks racing across the steppe: when you go back to where you were – it isn’t there ... not good or bad.…’

*

‘You – where do you go?’ she asks. ‘Where do your questions lead? Aren’t they a plea, and an excuse?’

‘I could be Jarrett,’ I say, trying to joke, ‘and hallucinate. I’m ill and helpless. I wheeze, can’t even wash my face.’

‘Well said!’ she says. ‘The Chinese answer, though – that is the one that promises the most for centuries, from now. Discipline, and fitting in: obedience, withdrawal. Work hard, take the rewards, luxury and opulence if possible, and don’t complain. There are professionals: they do the admin. It will be scientific, perfected, just like me. You won’t need bother, nor to criticise. Farm the resources, punish the transgressors, extend your influence and deals – then ... you hope it’s worth it, that it lasts, it doesn’t matter if it all does nothing good, and what is bad is covered up.... The species has no goal but a survival, growth, and harmony. Think honey-bees, how far ahead they are of us ... all those species, facing their extinction without fuss....’

‘I can accept,’ I say, ‘what you say, the Chinese protocol – it sounds the only way we have. It’s hard and realistic – not my world at all. Rich and poor, splendour and graft: hard graft. But, I realise too – science, perfection: I'm not into that at all.... It's good, Nesrine, that you are perfect and can decide what's to become of me.'

'Nothing will become of you,' she says. 'You are not here, not all of you, not enough to catch a hold. Mehmet, poor lad, he has doubts, uncertainties – but you are Doubt. You can't be told – it isn't strength or independence: it's not being here.

'All you can do, dear Alex,' Nesrine says, gesturing to Mehmet to be patient while she finishes me off, 'is breaking horses. Now, you realise, they wanted to be free. You put them in the market: those who submit, at least. They have shit lives, they're gelded, or have foals they never see grow up.... Pull carts, get thrashed.

'Everything you can do, you now reject. It's not your fault – another wasted life. We'll pick you over, like they filletted your dad ... I, and dull stupid Mehmet. It won't take long – we'll seize your loyalty and park you somewhere – the fall guy, ready to do jail-time, or to suffer the vengeance of some rival firm.... We are the founders of a tank. A thinking tank. Intelligence, Alex – it doesn't recognise a good or bad. Our enterprise will be crooked, it doesn't need to be, but that's how we are qualified. We'll know before the others think, before they see the silo's empty and the opium fields are poxed.

'You're of no use to us, but we can find a use for anyone: that is intelligence. Maybe we could use your skin, your bones – a bedspread or a xylophone...?

'But that is it. Accept – or not. It's of no consequence. That is the passage for us all ... you fantasised, that there was something more, and you could spell it out. You thought those nomad empires made of running water, waving grass, could be your way of life, your family: – as if they were your father, who created your body out of less than zero, and became your avatar. He passed on the grandeur of his hallucinations too. Not true. Not real. You took them on, as legacy.'

'Give me some work, Nesrine,' I say. 'I'll try to live with what you say ... I know you mean it as a cure.'

'Follow and trust neither the bad nor yet the good, Alex,' she says, 'don't persist in trying what you cannot do. Accept the mixtures that we have before us: good and bad were always luxuries, not on the market now. Remember ... each life is lived in vain, without a point....'

SEALS

'Help me close the ark,' says Nadine.

'It's not shipshaped,' I say. 'There's falling rocks, and here, if it floods, we'd all be drowned....'

It's a compound. We shoo the animals inside. They eye each other. It doesn't seem a happy place.

'If we feed them good,' says Nadine, 'they'll leave each other free.'

'Noah's dove,' I say. 'It could have found those olive leaves afloat, not growing, not on land. Besides, how'd you know where the land was. "There's land" – that's all. You don't know where the water goes – there's no enormous plughole, no cloaca maxima....'

'It's symbolism, Milo,' Nadine says. 'Hope. Families. Couples. Take precautions – build a boat and fuck the rest who aren't invited. Evil bastards, that's for sure.'

'Adam and Eve get left to drown,' I say. 'They had abundant symbols too, a clash ... don't mess with God: enough!'

'It's what Hitchcock had in mind – the movie with the gunshot,' Nadine says, flustered from beating bushes to unseat the waddling birds. 'And cymbals. Awake! Duck! There was a flood, they say – really, the water flowed out through the Bosphorus. Those "end of earth" stories you love to ponder through – there's always been them. The wrath of God, against the greed of man. You must love and trust, forget the anger – the boss knows best, trust Him. He loves you, though it's a close-run thing: you could drift for ever till the planks rot, if those birds aren't savvy....'

'The first humans,' I press on. 'Were made of mud. God didn't invent the wheel – some clever individual did that – he just used clay, slapped a lump, made a hominid, biforked, and then a woman, used his nail to make her cleft. They lived in mud houses, like we do – they've left no trace.

'It was the alcoholic father who couldn't steer, and his awful sons – they made the divisions: Muslim and Jew, black and white. And set the animals to feast on one another, to complete the pic....'

Nadine is angry. 'You love to go back, invent what isn't there, and long to live ephemerally, in places not like they're supposed to be, or never were.'

'So, what's wrong?' I ask. 'Think! The end of the world, the muddy, cosy world: when washed away, it grows; it's soil – wondrous fruits that smell of ambergris, tribes of apes swinging from the copra ropes they weave, living in green houses high above.... We'd all be friends. There's plenty, everything is plentiful. Community. Then comes the end, and start again –

extended families, feuding, monopolising the land, building in brick, creating lawyers, then the laws. The rules give property, in perpetuity: define the state, society, its gods ... the spirit of the laws, the good soldier and the renegade. We all must live by rules of possessing, added to what we know we need. The gods: a single God is unreliable, destroyer of creation. Those hominids, in His image, small and stupid, difficulty in standing upright. The pluri-gods, though are enterprising. Each against all ... men and women doing dirty tricks on everyone.'

'There's a goose under the lavender,' Nadine shouts. 'Take out the mash, and catch the stragglers.'

This, I do.

There's no angry God, no squabbling divinities. Just us. Is all that's left.

'Consciousness,' I say. 'It's all about that. Not who, not "who whom". Just keeping it alight. Once there was God – he blew it. It's us who shield the flickering flame....'

'Why?' she asks, looking for a contest. 'Besides, some places don't have a word for it, the difference: conscience or consciousness....? Does it matter if we're conscious without conscience? Can we be vice versa? Take Nazis ... conscious without conscience ... not conscious....? Stones, lichens? And yet – those move....'

'Mushrooms,' I say. 'They move, they don't resist. My favourite dish....'

'A vital spark, no more,' she says, throwing leggy pale things in a pot. 'They talk together, fungi do, just like the trees. But the world – it isn't set on fire by them, not like we've done. They're fine; they make the sacrifice to keep your intellect alive, and kicking out.'

'I'm off,' I say. 'Down to the sea.'

That dove – such discrimination, such a small bird too. I would have sent a vulture – to pluck an organ from a Parsee, a corpse atop a tower of winds – waiting to be purified. *That* would have been a sign of custom living; the dead laid out, mortality and cleanliness still alive.

'Take a stand,' Nadine says. 'I hate you being on the beach. Staring at nowhere.'

And here, with her, hatred is alive and seething, like the mushrooms in the pot – the poison driven out by fire, and foaming water.... Fear and loathing, to be disappeared.

There's the sullen sea. Gunmetal, a few white curls. 'Here,' says our neighbor. 'Take a spear.'

The wind brings them in – seals. On each wave, mottled, black-spotted, khaki, like gulls' eggs, a scientist's trusting, grandad face: a sparse mustache, a bloated body, blobby like a doodlesack dismasted, maybe a mewing sound – could be the wind, the crowd: some with their spears, darting in the waves, despatching. Another crowd – censorious, uncertain, watching, supporting.

I take a spear, don't use it. This is a cull – the monsters that eat the seals have themselves been eaten – probably by us. There's seals abundant, the spears go in, the sand is red. In Canada they used to club the white babies, the pups, no shedding blood, to save the fur. Now, each creature gets the spear, irrespective of its age, experience. There's no resistance.

It's nature. We're wading in it.

People need the protein, and it's thrown on to a cart. The horse trudges off inland – sometimes the smell of blood excites them. At mating time, they snap and bite each other. This horse is canny, silent, maybe tired. These huge slugs – the wobbly seal cadavers, a weight to drag over the sand and up the track. Day after day.

We are the guardians now, it's up to us to keep the balance. In the end, there's less and less to weigh. That balance, scales finer and finer, like jewellers use for tiny filaments.

The ark: no need of tanks, acquaria. The fish, the albatrosses, whales and such, they'd have survived innumerable, and ruled the world. 'Let it rain' – that is their anthem.... The seals – they must be starving, as we've eaten all their dinners, and they've overbred in hope: or profligacy. Or just – for nothing. Doing, being, what comes naturally.

I hand back my clean spear, go back to Nadine.

'They mustn't land,' she says. 'Or else they'd breed. Of course, it's not our element. It's a rule, the cull: like two by two.'

'A rule we don't observe,' I say. 'It isn't practical. It's a symbol, a binary ornament – like a mum and dad, two kids, to keep a steady state. Mind and body, heaven and earth. Two hands, two hemispheres, two ears....'

'Enough!' Nadine shouts. 'Eat. And sleep. That's another couple. Silence!'

*

'Let's go back,' I say to Nadine. 'Consciousness and conscience. Whatever the translations, things – including us – have consciousness but without a conscience. Or – we can ignore it. Some suppress both terms; absolutely. Others select where conscience has a place – where sex or money is involved, or politics, or killing people you don't like. Let's not quibble. There's a guy at work – he says even philosophy didn't establish what, if anything, a conscience was. It was religion did all that, and each religion has its sphere, rewards, does not communicate to disbelievers....'

That 'guy at work' – is me. Nadine won't start an argument with me, I win them all – by casuistry.

'Are you sure?' she asks. 'Your work is full of paradoxes. You say you're a risk assessor – but it's really probabilities. and there are lists, books full of sums....'

'I know,' I say. 'We tell the clients they're insured "against" – but really they're insured *for*, for something drastic, fearful, happening. The problem is – we ship,

ship everything; transport. We say we know how, that we have experience. But we don't – we don't know anything. We run a book, we bet – and if you win and things go wrong for you, you claim, we try to cheat you. It's a complex thing. And where does conscience enter in?'

'Maybe it doesn't, Milo,' Nadine says. 'Stop it! I'm better educated, better read than you. You won't solve the conundrum. Do your work, come home and put the animals I've saved in pens. The ark. Don't think of pens for writing – there's no future there.... I know – you wonder, wonder about the goddam seals. They lost their bets, they lost everything. Conscience doesn't come in with them. They don't ship freight, they don't take planes or go on cruises. Forget them – remember, now – they're food. Someone's bet's come up. "Flippers in blubber sauce" on the menu – an abundance!... Conscience? Well, perhaps it's good to kill, dismember, to save our lives. We believe it, anyway. I'm skeptical … it doesn't matter what I think.'

'The guy says, sometimes, intending to do bad, the outcome's good. Or half and half....' I say.

'Exactly so,' Nadine says. 'You'll have a list, a book, a file, that gives you an idea of consequences, the "maybe unexpected good" result. It doesn't count. You do the work, and do the sums, and only hope – like everybody else.'

'I'm troubled, Nadine,' I tell her. 'About everything. The book, those tables – it doesn't take me into its account.'

*

Forget the good and bad – just think of conscience, where does it apply? Vandalism – no accident: it's the will. Suicide – classed, and classed as good or bad? Genocide, was God's work in the flood ... there's agent orange ... coups d'état and rigged elections ... terror. Depends on who you are – maybe these are friendly fire.... I guess there's an arithmetic we could apply, but conscience, in the process, disappears.... When conscience decides what's good, or bad – what comes after, next?

'You're right, Nadine,' I say. 'You don't need it, not at all. Conscience is a paradox we can ignore. It's good to use it, but there aren't criteria, or consequences.'

'I misled you, Milo,' says Nadine: 'As if: we act "as if" we'd weighed things up, although we know – the outcomes can't be weighed at all....'

'That sounds like dynamite,' I say. 'Explosive....'

But – she's pounding mash.

She's clipped the geese's wings to keep them close, they huddle round our door, waiting for their feed.

She doesn't know – how I don't go into town to work. Nearby, there is a bar, I work from there; by midday I am high, less troubled too.

The mathematics. You need a nimble mind to get to it – but where was it before, eternal, lurking complete somewhere, internationalist and anti-colonial, gender-blind, without identity, coloured skin...? Huge, probably, an elephant of air, we feel a stringy tail and guess the rest. Where? Where is it? You use it as a vehicle – yet it gives solutions....

'You could work with animals,' Nadine says. 'Otherwise – you ask the questions you can't answer, nor can anyone. Your life is futile. Futility at the highest stage, but nonetheless.... And – you're in arithmetic, not mathematics.'

'I looked to you to sort things out, Nadine,' I say. 'You have this little refuge, it does for you, it doesn't resolve.... Endlessly, you prepare against the flood – what if it's fire? A virus? Or a bomb?'

'I know;' she says. 'An ark's a gamble, but – it is enough. But you – you don't know if you're full, bottled up, and can't let anything out at all: what if you're empty? It must be anguishing. The sensation – probably it's the same, full, empty: stuffed, barren: obese, skeletal.

'You remember, at first, we'd me: I used the image of the Klein bottle about you – the surface that looks as if it could contain, and be a banal, a joy-filled, stoppered bottle, but.... It's all a one; inside and outside; empty. A surface. Continuous. Endless. Terrifying.'

'In one respect,' I say. 'I'm terrified. You're right. We all are. You shouldn't seek a cure. The question is: "What do you do?" Not "What are you?"'

'We could stay here, as we are,' she says. 'You're welcome. I suffer for you, with you.'

'Thanks,' I say. I mean it, both as thanks and as reproof.

*

The universe, and all of us, are that surface; rolling out, unstoppable, bodies and consciousnesses. Some bottle! Someone cares for us, rocks were thrown an age ago ... they think that's how life came in from nowhere: space.

*

'Nothing to do with counting animals,' I say. 'Classifying them – two of each – should be enough. I's already taken care of.'

'You're ideal to work on risk,' the boss guy says. 'There's no other job in store. We don't do transfers. Everywhere's full up, except where you are, and that is at an end. The contract's up. No risk in that. You want another country ... a different start that has a different finish? Why did you think to come? And having come – want to move on, to somewhere undefined...?'

'Nadine and I,' I say, 'reject this place. The way it's been set up, its history that we don't believe, the society we wouldn't want to join. Nadine's answer is to talk to animals. Me – I'd turn it upside down, the whole place – have the documents fly up like larks, the cash out of your suits: your convenience, your stories – up, up and away. Up, and burn. Disappear, when gravity's run out.

'Nadine – we do well without each other, but together, our dislike, scepticism, boredom with you guys, boss types, all we must depend on, it provides us with a bond. We share hatreds.'

'I'm sorry for you,' says the boss. 'Sorry to see you go. We made you undergo a lot – I know it was hard, not what you were used to. It must get to you – calculating the worst – the predictable. Knowing how often you were wrong, and left uncovered.'

'No condescension,' I say, loudly. 'No apologies, no fake identities. Don't pretend I'm a Lakota or a Kurd, don't give me a colour or a sex, don't talk round me, fetishise me, romanticise, don't give me charity. Don't discriminate, don't forgive me for not being you, and don't reward me for it....'

'No,' he says. 'There's no need for that. Your time is up. You must have known, it was written and you signed it. Now, you're free, no one is over you. You took the risk, and you were exactly right. No transfer, no extension. Goodbye by contract.

'It's good – people expect that things change, improve, go the way they want, surprise them ... but you *know*! It's in the tables. You knew your time, exactly, to the minute. When you can calculate the risk, the time –

there is no risk. There's certainty. Now – live with that. What's next? Aha! That's where this theory fails – first, you must act, and only then can we weigh the consequence....

'Uncertainty – if you dither, there's no calculation. Is there risk? Of course! But it's incalculable.'

That's worth writing down. I wish I could pick out uplifting things – some generalities. How fantastic freedom is, how truth beats power, or maybe not. A quote, a flourish, nutshell, framed: or magnetised on a fridge door. Nothing. Futility. Fine words make reputations, and win cash.

Dirty thoughts – win nothing. Stay in your brain, and can't be sluiced away.

*

'It's true,' Nadine says, 'I remain a carer. Without me, the animals wouldn't starve, but they'd eat each other, one by one, until there was one left. What would that be? A grizzly? Not you, Milo. Without you and your arithmetic, nothing in the world has changed. We have no money. What will you do? Draw? You can't. Write? About the animals? A genre that's overcrowded, and will pass away. Write about people? Just for now, people aren't interested in others not like them, or struggling to resemble them; ingratiating – the poor, the wretched, the displaced – the neighbour that you didn't want, but they come anyway, become your family, and procreate....

'You can't do that, my dear, and if you could, you'd fall before competitors who've studied how.

'That leaves you a career as a keeper in a zoo. Cleaning up. Some nurturing. It's not, you think, why you strived to learn to read and write.'

'This is an artifice, Nadine. What you do – the ark, like zoos – a simulacrum of a natural life that's long long gone,' I say. 'And then, behold, the flood. But virtue, destiny – those no longer work when floods arrive. All's swept away, like you and me.... If I were a bandit chief, or sold drugs to the villagers – it's all the same. There is catastrophe, or not – it's all the same, the preparation for it and the consequence – it takes your whole existence.... There's no speculation – nothing that promises a fortune. With a flood – there's no speculation, and no cash.'

'A flood?' she says. 'With those, you used to have a contract. A compact. They've all expired, like yours; they don't make them any more.'

'When contracts die,' I say, 'there's tacit renewal. Who do we rely on? Not on me, Nadine, I'm gossamer, I'll blow away, if it suits. Anyway, it won't flood here. There'll be something else. It will come....'

'And be worse,' she says. 'An ark takes organising. The work implies reward – at least survival. What's worse than a flood?'

'It's here already, I am sure,' I say. 'Having no income's just the start....'

'You haven't understood,' she says. 'In the Book, the flood is good. Not just necessary, a punishment and reward, but good confirmed, over and over. Luck, signs – all demonstrate, there's a design, and things go on. There's breeding, and recovery....'

'I imagine we could farm,' I say. 'We might strike oil, although it seems all rock.... That story – the flood – big families, a few selected animals – it's not an origin, it's a re-birth of our reality, our civilisation. Disaster once more. We'll find we're in the same dead end – big families, closed in. Begin again, with nearly zero. A minimum of animals – the rest left to themselves, poached or fried.... Surely we could try another way, or are we stuck in stories circular, reactionary...?'

We stare at one another. What resources do we have? And what ideas? We won't flood here, so how can we prepare...?

*

There is no answer. There is no way out – no dove, no raven, crow, in flight. No flood. No happy ending, nor a sour continuation: no Architect manipulating us, no blueprint, no commercial centre.

We could invent. A road-show, a petting zoo. Incongruous. Become guerillas? – even be the first, becoming statues of ourselves: gorillas? None of this, not yet. Nadine ought not have talked of arks – it gives a depth, a background, we can't fill.

We wait. The animals – they low and snarl, cheep, grunt. It doesn't help, not them or us.

*

There's suffering, we argue, fight. But we survive. Change the scene.

MAISOON

To do a favour for my friend Issouf, I am to marry her, Maisoon, his friend. Mock marriage – gets her a passport, and the right to stay just where she is. Or else a right to go where she is not or never thought to be.

'We came through, Issouf,' I say. 'Me and Nadine; and that was it, the end. Everybody had hard times, until we knew hard times were normal times, and so – they weren't hard at all. We two – we left each other, when we had come through, and sighted land.... My trouble always was – I wanted to be loved for what I am. You're usually loved for what you do. May do. It's my pitfall. Nadine – she didn't love me for myself – that always changes, naturally....'

'That isn't so,' says Issouf, my friend, the best there is. 'In Algeria, in the Maghreb, Tunisia – what you are is what you stay, and how you start. It's Biblical,

Qur'anic ... no psychoanalysis, no story, no development. Forget you had psychology – you won't need it here. We know what you are, and you don't change and nothing changes you. You're committed to Maisoon, and she will love you, hate you, for yourself. Maisoon – best friend to both of us – who needs our help, especially, Milo, your complicity. You don't need do anything, have anything happen to you – for her, you are yourself and only you. You have to live with that. It's very hard, it's natural, so it's easy too. It's watching all the others – the people, the family – that erodes you, unless you're very hard. You're all at sea together, they know you for yourself, you can't get off, they see exactly what you are.'

'I came from here,' I say. 'Not here on the map, but somewhere similar.'

'We all do,' he says. 'But mostly it's forgotten. You, Milo, can't forget, and you remember things that happened before you were born, were settled. Now, you have the interview. You'll get the job, of being you, there is no pay, and you must pay – in every way, and every day.'

'You're formalistic, Issouf. You're a guidebook – something to read before you reach the place, which is quite different,' I say.

*

I miss, or, better, I regret, the animals. They brimmed with consciousness. They knew when we did bad by them – that's all you need to show you have a conscience. So many killed, futilely: those great extinctions. One feels sentimental, it happens to us all, it's written in the tables: there's no risk when risk is calculated right.

'Nowadays,' says Issouf, 'you have to think – can you support confinement? A prison. If you do bad, or you're somewhere where bad's being done – that's what you risk. Not physical pain, that's over quick if you have something to betray, know something, and worse if you do not ... but emptiness. Life taken away each minute, without end.'

'Imprisonment's the best,' I say. 'Agreed. Familiar, indefinite, and full of rules. Then, there's the big things, the bombs, the camps, the weapons: beyond imaginings, worlds' ending.... Prison is the best. It acknowledges your consciousness: it plays on it – a fortepiano, tuners at the ready. The rest, the executions, cops and soldiers, the torture and the inquisition – you don't know when or where. Prison is all around, it leaves you free to suffer on your own, have your own place of suffering.

'Being spied on – there's hypothesis, extrapolation. It's brain-work, that's for sure ... That too's around us every day, aimed at the brain, at everyone's, even those not on the roundabout. If you're a blob, lying on a dish – if you have a brain, you are desirable, a target....'

'You're wrong,' he says. 'There's no discussion, no exchange. Not with the law, not with the machines, not of the kind you want. Discuss with friends, that's all. If you can trust your friends. It's called academic: "philosophy". Only others similarly primed can understand – you speak "as if". What if? What might be done, has not been done, and almost certainly won't be – and if it is, it's not because of you at all. Friends, that's why you need them. Everybody else – they don't understand your rules. You, Milo, are rooted in hypothesis – what you say is what you might believe, but probably you won't. It's never taken so – you confess with every word, and anyone who confesses, you and they must know, is guilty, guilty of something larger that will eventually come out....'

'Perhaps, Issouf,' I say, 'the risk with Maisoon is too great – for me, for her ... before we start, before I take the test.... Any test we take, it tests some others; ... shared thoughts are a conspiracy.... Shared plans are military alliances.... Marriage, a bureaucratic ploy, would mean a document – trust and affection cost more than I have ever had. Most people are like me – shallow and changeable....'

'Love, affection, all that stuff – the sentiments,' he says, 'are not autonomous. They're creatures that will age: promiscuous by nature. They've been bred for different things, for digging, fighting, shouting insults.... Ask Maisoon, not if she trusts you, as of course she can't, but if she trusts the sentiments. Climb out your life, Milo – don't climb into someone else's. Lives aren't trees, and we're not monkeys.'

'I'm a spider monkey, Issouf,' I say. 'I'm threatened, nearly extinct. And I'm against history, not because it is the past, but because it is the ocean, most of the world, the context, habitus – why most things turn out different and reactionary from what I want, and anything I want to do myself. Maisoon is full of history, for sure – I'm not, but it means that I'm a husk, nothing but a skin, a rug, covering me, and not adhering.... All you see.'

*

I would have braved the wrath of God – He used to read you through your eyes, or maybe just – was canny. Now, the Flood is desolation, our fault, no redress, no cure, no confession or repentance. I saw that out – although there was more tide than flood, more submersion than a spate.

Maybe Maisoon could be de-natured, made like Issouf, less than what she is. A document. I won't assist in that.

'This is crap,' she said. 'There's everybody warned to welcome our accord. The white horse is booked, the feast....'

'That's Tlemcen, Maisoon,' I said. 'I can't ride – to teach me would take years. Besides, you all live here in Paris.... forget what is unreal, accept that we are friends, accomplices – and strangers too …'

'It's the thought,' she said. 'Relationships are bricks. They are a task – of adding one to one, not making two, and maybe even less than one.'

'That's old stuff, Maisoon,' I said. '*De l'amour*. Play the odds, don't touch the structures – it was futile.... Pretence and scheming, dead of the clap or by duelling on cliff-edge.'

'It's right,' she said. 'No one wants that. And you look stupid on a horse.'

'We should learn again to live in packs,' I said.

*

'Hyenas,' Issouf says. 'Eaters of dead flesh ... delimitated social orders ... and the antelopes don't gang up on them when they attack. Hyenas take a big beast down – it's placid and its mates look on – they stare ... the eating starts.'

'Enough of animals, Issouf,' I say. 'It's false. It isn't about them at all. How would the kangaroos get home from Ararat?'....

We laugh.

'I know I'm ridiculous, Issouf,' I say, 'but one ridiculous grain of sand in a sandy desert which is all ridiculous – what does that signify? Put it down to transition – always a difficult age. Seldom it ends in adulthood....'

'We Touaregs,' he says, 'maybe we're serious and end up stupid. Our many-headed struggle – is to make a territory that wavers like a cloud over where we are, or ought to be.... Not a state, not a solution – just what we want, our flag, our convictions ... our place.'

'It's a hard regime,' I say.

I mean there's lots of deaths.

'There's always deaths when you contest a territory,' he says.

'The French won't rest until they've got you on your knees,' I say. I think of those hyenas. Back off: nationalities are so sensitive. Just thinking gets you on a watch-list.

'And them, who're winning all the wealth, invisible, but on the maps....' I say, and think how Touaregs won't dig it up, but someone else will have the contract ... leaving all the other people, scrabbling, submitting, without the faith....

'And faith. Some have it, I am sure, but mostly, it's a flittering ... and then there's raids and dirty deals....'

'Oh,' he says. 'You should read a book about the Bonaparte – Well! What he tried to do without the faith! And how they fought on and on for centuries, when he was beat! And fought and lost and sometimes won ... the lesson isn't clear ... except, a brutal power....'

'You don't want to go down that track....' I say.

Clearly not. He draws a web of tracks – with a fingernail on the café cloth, making furrows that fill in and disappear – the cloth is worn and blotched.

'It will go on all your life,' I say, 'and mine, and all our lives, here and there; all the lives laid end to end and moving fast, forward and back, and very tough. I guess what you have now anyway remains: precarious and poor, but maybe getting less, new people swarming round with nothing, nothing to do or trade or farm, and the sun roars each day as if you're falling into it.... Discipline intermittent and archaic, and roaming here and there, a hungry beast....'

He guesses I am on his side, but – my talk's a cloud; or mercury in blobs, escaping, pooling.

I say, 'About Maisoon – it's pretty trivial, as if some way it made a difference. I don't set store on feelings, especially not mine.... On promises, still less.'

Issouf should have something that he wants: his flag, a wind to wave it in.

The cops are everywhere, and they tell tales. There's spying old and new. Being on a side, or none – it seems to make no difference to how you end. Once you're on, there's no way of getting off the list. Guilt or resistance – they both wear you down. It's foolish of them, but they know who you frequent – not what you think.

'Of all the stupid things,' says Issouf. 'Your story with Maisoon has the record. Too bad there is no prize. You're archaic, Milo. How you think, how you act. Look round....'

Everyone is staring at their telephones, even the background music's been turned off, so they can hear the tiny sounds....

'Azawad,' I say. 'The Sahel. That sounds archaic too. Your identity, and mine – strips of gummy paper hanging off the wall. We are resisters....'

'We are occupied,' he says. 'You're not.'

*

'Do you see all of us who're sitting here, as soldiers? You might treat them so, in war....' I say.

'I think you're looking for a different nationality,' Issouf says. 'All of you. You'll maybe all end up as Chinese. Not me! You want to win, be on the winning side at least, you think it's easy, you just choose right and so it all turns out. You'll be disappointed, even if you win. Especially if. But no – you're not all soldiers – you're in an army, a modern one, where there's computer guys and scientists and armourers and publicists. Hardly anyone does fighting, mostly you're trained you shouldn't hate, not discriminate – kill from afar, according to the law.

'You don't know who is who, or why. I may get in your way, the wrong place ... just standing round, just looking on. You can't tell if I'm on the other side. Perhaps you'll pay me to betray – don't trust me, though. There's no quick ending....'

'Words,' I say. 'You trump one with another word. The pack is large, two hands can't hold it, shuffle it. There is no bank, there's only other words. That's what you play with, and play for. The suffering doesn't come through words. Making the table and the chairs, printing the cards – that's suffering. You can lose along the way – lovers, illusions, children had, not had, your muscles, your blood turning white – cream cheese – your sight, your voice, your plausibility – God and his devil in their carriage, driving off at a fork, you won't see them again unless they double back, an ambush – all that, you lose, your tranquillity, your cash, and don't know who has got it all ... you're used to losing, but in the end, at the last – you cling. Cling to yourself, the nameless part which once enabled all the rest....'

'It isn't words,' Issouf says. 'Those are rote, no longer written down. You can't add to them, they're memory. It all blows away, everything; the others, comrades, teachers – you see them reddish-yellow in the wind, and then all is gone ... except what you stand on and the vast land in front of you, empty and burning, pricking your feet, your eyes, like thorns.'

'Once you have learned a few of them,' I say. 'Words may sweep away the suffering – there's contiguity instead: "death" comes next to "deaspirate", God follows "go-cart". And there's roots: "following" makes "execute' .... Roots, approximations, chance: they made you walk upright, alas, and they take over. You lie down. That's it. Flat.'

'You're good with speech,' Issouf says. 'And you'll watch while people, less articulate than you, will hunt me down.'

'Not you,' I say. 'People like you. Because on balance it must be done. For the sake of everything that won't be changed if you are gone.'

'"Gone"?' he says. 'Cities "go". People don't. If you've ever been alive, you know that everything always changes, you can't stop it, bodies get in the way.'

*

'I'll be a communicator,' Issouf says. 'I've no intention to have a gladiator's death.'

When they catch Touaregs, they blind them, tie them in line and have them wander off. In the past, blinding caused death, they say, but now, there is a laser gun – it burns out your sight. Each morning I saw the scholar-physicist who had won the grant to work on this – defensive, a precaution, that's what they say. Blinding: it's a deterrent, if you believe in life but not in paradise, where everyone is blind and deaf, knowing all that needs to be.

'They must not procreate.'

'You're indeterminate,' Issouf tells me, 'by your innocent name. But the question isn't indeterminate. It's sending armies out: they'd scarce decamped, they'd left their rubbish: and here they come again. Obedient and keen.'

*

'Winning or losing; risk: it doesn't affect at all what you do.... I have always been a revolutionary....'

'Why are you telling me this rubbish?' Maisoon asks. 'I know you're useless. You let me down, for futile reasons – here comes more futility.

'You were right to do a favour by saying farewell to me. European men – "Angles" – quite useless for three hundred years, after the extermination wars. You were spent, once you'd decided who was God and how to get to heaven. All you had since, is money, mis-earned from others....'

'I have new ideas,' I say, improvising.

'You had the document I need,' she says. 'Priceless. That's why we were inseparable.'

'No, Maisoon,' I say. 'I never had the document. I had money, and when it went, I did not exist. I was glad. I had work once, but it's all slipped away. Goats. You end up two by two. Confined, while the rain lasts, and then you're meat.'

'If I'm not legal, they won't take me on the ship,' she says, deflated. 'I'm sure I'd make it as a pioneer. Mars. Getting away from here, being the founder of somewhere different.... I'm small enough to fit in to the ship, big enough to last the trip.'

'Just think,' I say. 'You could be the first illegal: landing on Mars, without a passport. You all would be.'

'That's not a good thought,' she says.

'When I worked,' I say, 'I was irregular.'

'When you worked, Milo, you were drunk,' she says.

'The sans-culottes ate bad,' I say. 'The revolutionary *plat républicain* had to be washed down with pints of red. Lots ended up on their documents, and in their minutes.'

'Writing things down,' she says. 'It's a giveaway. You can't get over that: and can't deny.'

'I have my bad side too,' I say. 'Not all pleasure, goodness, and fervour. Those who God decides to save are those who aren't a threat to Him. You could say he's lenient on the powerful bad, tough on the silent good. Badness gets you to Brazil, Argentina, sometimes the Vatican.'

'God doesn't like people who want to change the world He's made,' she says. 'That's why going to Mars is a solution. On Mars, there's room to set up anything. That way I can keep the faith and cock a snook.'

'If we didn't speak in metaphor,' I say. 'We wouldn't speak at all. Our lives are terrible. If there's not eternal sun, there's everlasting rain.'

'You know who is to blame for that,' she says. 'It's what there was before, the past that set the future up; there was blame but written down on scraps, like pass the parcel.... You can't blame God, it must be something bigger that comes after that....'

'You can't have blame without identifying badness,' I say. 'If we're not the bad ones – then who is? The people who are punished? No one blames the poor for poverty, not now ... the wretched for being wretched....'

'Well,' she says, 'that's comforting.' We laugh, we smile, at least.

'If I don't believe in God,' she says. 'What then? Who takes the rap? Us? Capital? Fortuna?'

'Run, Maisoon,' I say. 'You're far behind the field.... The penalties have all been handed out.... No time has yet been served.'

I couldn't talk to Nadine like this. I'm not sure that it's good.

The animals – maybe they are metaphor now, have always been – though now we can replicate their meat in petrie dishes, we'll only need a small one for the house ... our companion ... bark and purr ... enough!

Creation has passed: a one-off. So has the old-time wayfaring, in sandals, on horseback, or in hulks.

Once there was the movement, the Organisation – if it wasn't for you here, then somewhere else. Then came the floods, flood after flood. Lots of people, struggling, two by two: and isolation, loneliness.

A new dispensation. Maisoon would say there's been a coup in heaven – some new guy, stark and childless, a masturbator, enforcing novel rules. Stay where you were, sleep alone, don't get ideas.... It's a thought! Fascists – they never tire. They're in those rice-grains, the embryos ants carry round, reproducing without end. Termite cities. If a sentient force created everything, it will have been a fascist; its image on the coins....

*

'I could do cabaret,' says Maisoon. 'Get a following. A flame in the dark. Trying something I know is too difficult for me – but I *know* it is.'

'Yes,' I say, enlightened. '"Gardens where a lone jet of water burns among the stones at dusk..." That's you!'

How I love you, Maisoon. Vanity, vanity....

'Most people like you, Milo,' Maisoon says, 'died long ago. You're quite a miracle.'

'If you break with your inheritance, you'll be disoriented,' I say, 'but you'll be free.'

'Yes,' she says, 'and you have no inheritance, Milo. You can see what that means for you ... No freedom, and no cash.'

'Oh,' I say, 'I invented the flourish. That freedom – it's mine, my creation. Without me, it doesn't mean a thing. My promise – you are free of it. It was my device to keep you close ... protected, one of us. I'd hoped it could be done. I couldn't guarantee you wouldn't drown, you, your family tree submerged, the last branches with your cousins clinging – maybe they saw the tattered birds above, dancing in circles.... It's the names, that are the giveaway. Abass, Munira: they could have chosen different.'

'You can't stop there, Milo,' Maisoon says. 'Train me. Teach me to be an astronaut. Flying to the stars. If you can't give me a culture – compromise. Teach me to be a traveller....'

'If you're an astronaut,' I say, 'you don't go to the stars. It's more mundane, much closer too.'

‘I must get away,’ she says. ‘They’re all driven, the astronauts – criminals, awaiting trial, guilty of terrible things – they think in the ship their awfulness will be forgot, they’ll be born anew when they return, cleansed, purified....’

‘You’d live there with them in the ship in total promiscuity,’ I say. ‘For some, it’s their fantasy. You’ll find, when they take off their suits – the tattoos will show what’s in store for you, and battles between you all! – it often happens that a ship will dock with all the crew slaughtered, en route. You realise, I hope, there’s nothing that you’ll find out there. It’s all been mapped – the only risk is when you land and maybe can’t take off again. That’s the experiment, to see who will survive ... otherwise, who cares? These clouds of gas with rocky chips like Spanish nougat ... a hectare of the Congo has more precious stones than all of Jupiter .... Expect no memorial – forgotten, discarded, if you should survive, unreported if you don’t....’

‘That, I’ve been told,’ says Maisoon. ‘It’s evident. And if you hit a star, you’d frizzle up. But – it’s my destiny....’

‘We start, my dear,’ I say. ‘By studying the birds. Flight. The dove, discovery – the promise of a settlement – impregnable, a mountain, a fortress, even if there’s no one who threatens.... You’re armed, of course, but shoot only when you land. Before, you would explode the craft....’

'The human side,' she says. 'Yes. That's what I need. The forty months or forty years they close you in – there's scientific stuff to do. It's all pretence.... Down there on earth, it's all decided anyway.

'I need to know what it can take to get away, and find another land, and maybe stay....'

'It's not like that,' I say. 'You must be reconciled. You make the voyage – times indeterminate, and dangers all around. When you arrive, you must return at once – or possibly you make a camp, and see if life's supportable ...you and your mates... Mates! With strange languages, assigning fiddling tasks without autonomy, reward ... and off you go again. My dear – the climate ... boiling seas and stinging sands....'

We laugh.

'At least,' she says, 'there could be a cage: canaries. Or some parakeets – a jolly pig, a nimble gecko....'

'It won't be recognised,' I say. 'Your sensibility, your sense. Take me. With Nadine, we saved the animals, on land, day after day ... and then, and then....'

'I had a similar experience,' she says. 'I came from Africa to here by land – extenuating, but it saved us from the sea. Water – if only all whose habitat it is could live free from net and trawl and industry....'

'I could show you how to go from here up to the moon by land,' I say. 'There is no sea until you get there, then – the Sea of Dreams, it's called. No one has ever been there. That, at least, is true: no one has ever been into their dream....'

We ponder this. 'There's books that contradict,' she says 'And did they see? – the moon, thronging with monstrous life, the angels: and the sea of blood, dividing, swallowing the troops, the tanks. Intelligence consumed....'

We laugh some more: then, 'You're right,' she says, 'It's quite ridiculous, this journeying through space, in boxcars filled with wires, or coracles with muzak.... Space is waiting there, for us to fill it with futility....'

'I told you, you will not be recognised,' I say. 'Not reason, nor your personality. Nor everything you won't be able to accomplish.'

Always the same voyage, same trip. We who make it to the other shore – our skill and bravery are not acknowledged ... indeed, we're sent back to try it all again.

'And the animals?

'The animals, Maisoon? You wonder how they ended up, when we abandoned them. They wander off. They're animals, of course. Voyages don't mean anything special to them.'

'Important things will happen in Algeria,' she says. 'And neither of us will witness them.'

'No white horse for me in Tlemcen?' I ask, amused. 'I'll not be bridegroom, but a sombre cavalier. Siegfried rode a white horse….

'You and I, Maisoon, we've seen death, separation, affection – we started at the end, now there's just the two of us remain ... pristine, at the beginning....'

‘Then nothing,’ she says. ‘Like at the start. We didn’t know each other. We won’t.’

It’s true – there’s no consolation in reaching ends.

*

We say that only humans need or can feel guilt. Responsibility for what the robots and the algorithms do – that too is layered and assessed, an artichoke of choices and disclaimers....

*

‘I’m Mister Tod,’ says Kemal: Kemal is not his name, not really, just a tribute to a passing master. ‘Tod hunts, is hunted,’ he goes on. ‘That is me. What are you? Mister Dodgy?’

‘No,’ I say. ‘Someone did a favour. I have a contract. Even in war, especially ... you need insurance. I came to assess the risk, and put it, all our lives and actions, into ringing coin.... Mister Tod, the foxy one – it’s a misnomer: behind you there is death; Todt.’

‘We were a band,’ he says. ‘Defend the neighbourhood, our friends....’

‘You have a cause, Kemal,’ I say, ‘and you have the backing of a foreign power, a contradiction ... of what you want to be....’

‘Master Todt,’ he says. ‘That is our backer.’

'The frontiers, Kemal,' I say. 'I'd hoped to find a way ... my lover, in a sense – I could ferry her back home, but the border's closed. Suspended for the nonce.'

'Teach her to fly,' says Mister Tod. 'There are no planes. You dodge the nets, and find a perch, and then ... the urge, to find another place, another season ... off you must go. It's natural, always be prepared for flight – a mating, nest, a search for warmth. They shoot at you – still, you can go everywhere, even if it's where you are expected and not wanted. *You* expect, *you* want. You can't want otherwise, and you will go, fly to where your trip will end.'

'And then?' I ask.

'Home,' he says. 'On water. Or in a tree. Me? – back with the vixen, underground.'

'Those big white cars, like angels drive,' I say. 'Expensive dogs.... The risk is high. That's very good. The premiums ... too high?'

'The point is not risk high, risk low,' he says: ' – it's getting sums right, and premiums paid. Resist the paying out. You're soldiers, just like us. It's easy. It takes a day to learn. It's dull, that's all.'

'Shout and sing,' I say. 'No one will care what you have done – lose, you die; win – you're innocent again. It's easy, like you say. You take the risk – most people do, who can't avoid, or choose another insurer, another book of tables, a new actuary....'

'Risk isn't about reason, Milo, but you've found a way to bring in reasoning and consequences,' Kemal says. ‘Through that – responsibility, too – and guilt. But risk is not where we begin. Start from something else. Don’t teach her how to fly. If you are tired, you fall silent in the sea, it’s natural like your life, and no one knows you’re gone, or what you’re called, or what state powers have counted you, discounted and weighed you in no scales.... You have no counterweight,’ says Kemal, Mister Tod. ‘*We* signify. The fox, and maybe you. The common seabird’s just a fleck of paint.

‘You would-be communists,’ he says, ‘are full of conscience unexplained – so it can come and go....’

‘Everybody now is communist,’ I say. ‘Marx described a world in which conscience played no part at all. He expected Nazis – not socialism. No one’s capable of organising socialism, however simple that may seem.

‘Everybody tries to find a little bit of conscience. You guys, Kemal, you’ve thought it so significant, you made it into something watching you, over you, that doesn’t belong to you at all.’

Foxes hunt flightless chickens, penned, unguarded.

You must believe in foxes. They were a bother to us in the ark. They’re beautiful: do I believe in all the rest?

*

‘Well, Maisoon,’ I say, ‘all the countries now are blocked. We can’t move, not from one on to the next –

though countries move like tortoises that crawl on heaps of tortoises.'

'Forget it, Milo,' Maisoon says. 'Me – I want to leave, not to arrive. Forget me too. You'll move on to where there's no war, just jail and harshness. Don't waste your life in vanity.... looking for what's not.'

'I love vanity,' I say. 'And chance. Insurance is a nonsense, impossible. An illusion. There are good things you can be ... not for long, but it's still evidence. Here's one.... Being a big animal who's rarely eaten – every city's built to keep out hungry felines, and elephants. That's why they exist – otherwise, no one would live in them.'

'Honour, family,' she says. 'Silence. Those are rocks. You swirl around them, Milo. Useless. You don't understand; nothing is about what you should do, it's all always about doing what you're told. That's religion, politics, economics. You want a different setting – there is none. All you can do is build an ark. Bigger and bigger ones. It's charity, and your passengers won't thank you – they'll be seasick, and jump overboard, if you don't keep them locked down in the hold.'

'This is farewell, then?' I ask, knowing that it is.

*

I tried. It hadn't come easy or natural to me. A waste of time. Saving the world was difficult, finding a document for Maisoon impossible.

I'm lucky – I have been able to contemplate my death: a gazing at it day after day, and discussing which 'bang' will mean the world has ended. Every human has had this unique opportunity, once again.

So, forget Maisoon; forget good and bad – those will exhaust me. It used to be our claim, that distinguishing between them should let us lord it over all the rest. Too bad!

I paint the world in miniature – bright colours, but small enough to work as a tattoo; or chipped, slid beneath your top skin – won't hurt if it's cut out. Don't thank me, don't pay me, no recognition, it's all evidence, can be held against you or me or anyone. My world, my enamel brooch, my locket, a world made tiny – beautiful; though, like the foxes, eating all there is and more.

I hope you can appreciate....

*

'So, that was me, finished,' I say. Dorsa and Tawkiq stare at me. They're not of my confession. All three of us are drunk.

'I could do anything,' I say. 'Clean as a flying fish. No job – but within me, my awful skill – the numbers game. Insurance. If I must, I'll work.

'After a flood, there can be many floods. It doesn't prove a thing. Those plagues – they multiply – they're infinite. With science they grow smaller, more insidious.... more and more....

'All the disasters – once you could believe there's someone at the helm, someone who knows a destination, steers: gives you life sentences, makes you straight or bent. But now – we know how, at the best, it will go on. More conveniences, more of everything the same. Machines to be fixed, people patched; machines stripped down, people abandoned – depends on cash....

'The sea! Comes in your shack, perhaps, or gives you fun – protected immersion, then lying beside it on your rug.... Or – nothing. It could go badly wrong, they said: and if it did ... nothing can be done.'

'You're absolutely wrong, Milo,' Tawfik says. 'There will be many different types of human, shapeshifting, unpredictable. Psychology will flower – and the world will shake and slither like blancmange. your house, your hut, will melt around you while you sleep, the mountains become lakes, the glaciers will ramp up to the skies, it will be hot and cold, the plagues will multiply and come anew each day – we'll have to learn a new life every hour – the suns will procreate more suns, like they once did, the rivers will be gas, the deserts chocolate fudge ... not that it will be edible ... everything will look familiar and yet ... don't stick your finger in, don't taste unless it's labelled fresh that hour....'

'Well,' I say, 'at least we trust the labelling....'

'No, no,' he says. 'Our systems, our insides, our inside outs – they'll all be changed as well – some of us digesting grass – at last – and others chained to caviar with seconds of profiterolles. The labels will be useless to you if you graze on plantains and rosbif....'

'I don't believe it, Tawfik,' Dorsa says. 'I'm sure it's like what Milo says. All congealed, and still precarious – all in doubt, unchangeable.'

'Then fuck you, Dorsa,' Tawfik says, laughing hugely and drinking manhattans by the jug. 'If you don't share my vision, my reality, how can you share a part of me? Go with Milo here – see if his tables tell us what's to come.... I promise you – in the new world, you'll be in jail today, tomorrow on the gurney wheeled to execution – then a total pardon for some stupidity you thought, and you'll be made a colonel in intelligence, a prison governor – till next week.... We have regained our expertise in living on the earth, and have the body parts required to hunt and fish and do écartés in our sleep.'

He outruns both of us. We gawp. It's not impossible, what he says. 'And you, Dorsa,' Tawfik says, 'you are renounced. I fly....'

He flies! – he manages what I had tried to teach Maisoon, and had to leave her in the line outside some office where she'll plead her cause.

We leave the bar: Tawfik's truck awaits. 'Earth moved,' the side says. 'Pits dug and attics cleared. Pools cleaned, banks reinforced.'

'I have help, of course,' he says.

We all feel strong and pure. I put my hand on Dorsa's knee. She draws away and pinks me on the hand with her fag's end.

'You should apologise,' says Tawfik, who drives with great attention to the road, and all the rest that's fleeting by. 'You'll find that when things work as I predict, you'll be apologising frequently. Start now….'

I am dismayed, contrite. 'I'm not myself,' I say.

'That's the first step, it seems,' says Tawfik, as we reach their modest home.

There are two rooms, very small, more like closets – 'If you make these into one,' I say. 'You could both live spaciously....'

'There's space outside,' says Dorsa, laughing. 'Immense expanses. You can't just pull a piece off and put it in your house – besides, it's immeasurable, and every day there's more. You can't order what you'd like! Why would you want to destroy this cosiness – to simulate a voyage between stars....'

'You see,' says Tawfik, 'we forgot the bees and ants. the soldiers, the idlers, the leaf-cutters, the hive dwellers, the city-builders, the red, the black, the white ... some flock, some produce, some just flit and wander.... They persist, they flourish, despite all our attacks. We should be like them, accept and accentuate our differences ... but in the end.... Well, of course, the end's the end, whatever you have planned to do....'

'He's opposed to holy war,' Dorsa whispers, pulling me close in a tiny corner of a tiny room. 'He fought the jihadis in Burkina.... It was very hard....'

'We used to be much smaller,' Tawfik says. 'We could make our gardens, little plots of paradise, we were not observed. Who would observe us? Then we grew tall, and on our hind legs, taller still – we drew the attention of the gods, the religious started meddling ... good, bad, after death, watch out when you have intercourse – families and states ... the whole unwanted, the exorbitant, the shooting-match....'

'Yes, yes,' I say, delighted. 'That is my theme! I love you both so much, at last I've found people who think like me....'

'Well,' Dorsa says, as we three stand pressed together, there not being room to bend.... 'You haven't understood. No one thinks, will ever think, like you. Standing pressed together as we are – it isn't thought. Indeed, it's quite the contrary: the hive-been, termites – they don't think, all hugger mugger, locked together. If you want to think, you must go outside, forest, jungle – Tawfik will make a clearing for you, prune, remove some branches if you need to watch the stars....'

'What are we waiting for?' asks Tawfik, hail-fellowing.... 'A drink! Some home-brew, hooch? *Filu e ferru*' and he yanks the wire, and pulls a demi-john from beneath our feet.... 'Laid down before the flood!' he shouts. 'Last week, of course....'

It's true – the chipboard of the house is warped and damp. They're living well with the uncertainty – that's what the actuaries say. Our bodies warm the wood, there is miasma, shoots of rice and grain spring out.... 'Here's plenty!' Tawfik says. 'It starts and ends this way! Enjoy it, everything encapsulated, the universe in miniature.'

'I feel it's casuistry, Tawfik,' Dorsa says. 'If everything is part of everything, the start and finish is in everything, not just in this poky house, but in you and me, and this guy Milo too. You talk in platitudes, my dear, in sounds. Where do sounds go, when they're not audible? some vibes – go on and on, into infinity? Or just like us – they die, they do not leave a corpse but they are inaccessible for ever ... whether they're alive or really dead, or maybe for a sound, there is no difference ... like us, they're born to die....'

She weeps, though what she's said, and weeping too, are both a platitude.

*

We're sleepy. The grappa has invaded us, we're drunk and lucid. 'Quick,' I say. 'Before we drowse – we three, pressed close together here – what does it seem to you?'

'Yes, yes,' says Tawfik, 'you're quite right. It's like a space ship, not going anywhere – and yet ... like all the rest, the species – we are travelling at space-age speed, in space-ship confines on the earth – around, around we go! Around the sun we spin but never get there – what a pointless trip...! Not going anywhere but travelling faster than the speed of sound....

'If only one of us had known a would-be astronaut, who'd prize the experience we dislike – of being on the earth, in space, all pressed together ... round and round at breakneck speed....'

'Yes,' I say. 'I knew a dear friend – she could not find space on earth – wanted to be an astronaut, but couldn't find a ship for want of documents.... My dear Maisoon.'

'If only we'd have known,' says Dorsa. 'She wouldn't need her papers here.'

We sleep, and wake refreshed and lucid, on our feet.

*

'Today, I must make a garden,' Tawfik says. 'How shall it be, Dorsa?'

'A cold garden,' says Dorsa, 'keeps strangers out. And plant – pinks, parrots – and passion-fruit, in memory of Milo. Celandines, clematis, cyclamens and coriander. You get the idea. And a magic apple tree – I saw the picture.'

'I know what you have in mind, Dorsa,' says Tawfik, making a clearing in his head. 'Forget good apples and bad apples. It was a fraud: God planted it, concealed it, and punished us for finding it. Would you trust anyone who did that? What a shit!'

'It's intended as worldly wisdom,' I say. 'The point of being human is that only we know what is good and bad. And that we get punished, even if we know all that. Why? If it was a founding notion – ethics, morality – it was poor. Most people didn't know about the apples – Greeks, Romans, Indians, Chinese.... It's against reason and against practise. If you don't know about it, there's no punishment – except by happenstance and ill-fortune.... Slipping on the ice: that's punishment enough. If you know, God punishes you if you are bad, if He made you bad, bad apple. If He made you good, you made a slip! It's all will, of course. Don't care? Indifferent to good, and to evil if it doesn't light on you? You won't last forever, whatever you decide.

'Good apples still get bugs, they resist but intermittently....'

'That's more like plums,' says Dorsa. 'My experience is, one year they're abundant, and almost none the next.'

'Religion does not convince,' I say, 'unless you get what you have paid for, cash or kind. Science is a greater power by far, and is indifferent to the good – or bad. You have to trust the whitecoats, when they're brewing bombs, or making LSD. As for plums – I think I'll miss out the lean years, Dorsa. Maybe I'll go wandering, not seeing the same place twice....'

'Beware!' she says. 'Wandering means poverty. Besides – the settled people don't like nomads. The Han – they've fought, done deals, envied and persecuted those beyond the walls....'

'East Turkestan,' I say. 'It's always been a centre: you have to be, if you are in-between....'

'They're not real nomads,' Tawfik says, 'not for ages. The old-time ones had cities, written stuff – I have friends there.... I'll give you an address....'

'I thought you might come with me,' I say, my muscles cramped with grappa and with standing up....

'No, no,' says Tawfik, 'when we have got rid of you, Dorsa and I – we hope to split.'

That's an upsetting note.... 'I've always grown to hate the place I'm in,' I say. 'I must explore the world – exploration is all we have, nothing else survives or goes on making sense....'

'That's nonsense,' Dorsa says. 'The aim for all of us is unanimity, agreement about everything. Tawfik's a fantasist – people who don't fit are sick ... wandering off's the first sign of dementia, Milo. You must be caught, brought back.... Find you some work that stultifies, sedates....'

'We're a tight fit here, Dorsa,' I say, trying to wriggle and find space. 'Don't give me grappa, I feel it corrodes away my years, people to see, miniatures to prick into my skin....'

'If you're not good in Tawfik's garden, Milo,' Dorsa says. 'All the plants will die.'

We laugh.

'Are there many gardens, Dorsa?' I ask.

'They're all for sale,' she says. 'All the turf has been raced over. Full of energy and dreams.'

'Don't exaggerate,' I say. 'All grass is like that.'

Could anyone be bored by Tawfik and his Dorsa? I'm beginning to be....

'Jung says,' I begin, 'that someone led by rational judgment should be considered as driven equally by unconscious irrationality. That's really confusing, for a perfect, integrated couple like you two.'

'Not really,' Dorsa says. 'Turn us and turn about. It doesn't help the puzzle you have set yourself, whether one or both of us is good for you. Jung is a turf that's been raced over; now, only the losers still run on.

'You, Milo – don't be scared. You've taken care to have nothing about you anyone could covet. You want nothing, except the indescribable and the unattainable – no one will help you to get that. You're the introvert. Do you want me to analyse you, Milo? It's old hat and useless. It all comes down to symbols, your unconscious spat – the battle between two animals, two monsters.... It's out of this world! Unearthly!'

'I didn't mention symbols with you, Dorsa,' I say. 'What's problematic is not me, or you, or Tawfik. It's what we lived through, are in the midst of – and what's to come.'

'Sure, it's about us; and what we do,' says Tawfik, greasing a chain saw.

'Nadine wanted to conserve. You two have a business and are happy in this little house,' I say. 'Patience rules.'

'And you're reactionary,' says Dorsa, triumphantly: 'Racist, and sexist.'

'You may be right,' I say, thinking of all my clumsiness. 'Paternal with Maisoon as well....'

'Choose a side and fight for it,' says Tawfik, striding to his truck. 'Help me dig, Milo.'

We drive up a narrow logging track. 'Dorsa has lost her illusions,' Tawfik says. 'Most of them she passed to me.'

There are little clearings, the felled trees abandoned, grey and rotten. 'We make bowers, rather than gardens. Gardens you tend and argue with. Bowers – await a happy couple,' Tawfik says.

At day's end, he pays me off. 'You've become a complication,' is all he says.

*

Once you could cross the continents on animals – not on their legs, but through their furs. Trapping, selling them. Now, the trek is poor and hard: you trudge on metals: gold, cobalt, copper, nickel, iron. Miners – who don't dig. Paid enough to keep you moving on. Never meeting another Dorsa and Tawfik, simple and complex, bright and stupid.

In court on Mondays – for the weekend, being drunk, disorderly and threatening, in a line of sleepy Indians, innocent, some at home, all thinking of elsewhere, all moving on.

Mines, strung out in veins, exploding in bloody nights – this sketch defines the whole like Delacroix; his Morocco ... the slaves, executions, peppery colours, mustards, angry horses fighting till dawn.... That is the moment, history, unrepeatable: the tops.

Mines green with malachite, salmon, henna, luminous yellow, hot, freezing, anthracite, and dried bull's blood.

Ants' nests. Your life given up to all the comrade ants, you love them, maybe you are happy but no one thinks to ask – your soul in hell, everyone blind and acrobatic, all time a graveyard.

'When there's a melt,' I tell Toma, a dynamiter, met where I dig – 'all these holes, these mines, will be filled in. Perhaps they're drains. They wouldn't tell us – we're not valued, but we're needed.'

Toma's my shift boss – he tells Smilga, the manager, about the melt.

I made a mistake.

'You're welcome to the melt,' says Smilga. 'Opinions differ. You're wrong, Milo – and besides, you can change your mind. But – you can't go from mine to mine, agitating, calling for a remedy which means us changing everything. Stopping the mine? New ownership? Your contacts, your associations ... we've all swallowed some communism now, but you're a different type....'

I think of Dorsa, she and Tawfik as two animals, two monsters even.... They are all you need, all you will find, in human types. Can monsters swim? We never had them in the ark.... Those tiny gardens, for sale, more unfinished stories, until they're overgrown and disappear. Crows will eat the apples.

'It's not ideology, Smilga,' I say, 'or propaganda. I survived a flood, remember. I ask you, what shall we all do when it's impossible to carry on as we did?'

'I could put you on the list,' he says, 'so you wouldn't work in mines, not in this continent. But where'd you go after? Where do martyrs go? You drag a tail of consequences after you.'

'It's about water, Smilga,' I say, 'not change. Water will flow where it wants, where it can. It doesn't think about us, it has no imagination. That's all, that's my point. My starting point.'

I lie. A melt would be immense. I wouldn't care, I'm not responsible. Let everything happen. When everyone is on the list – *that* is the melt. We've won? I've not won anything, I'm not there. I've been warned, and warnings mean the step's been taken. Where shall I be?

*

'I feel at fault,' says Toma. 'As your shift boss, I'm your guardian, and I shopped you to the management. You're ill-informed but too inquisitive.... Have you never wondered why our mine's so spacious...?'

'I know about space,' I say, 'and mines are confined, enclosed. All the shiny stuff's been taken out, smelted, poured away as molten slag – and yes, what's left are vaulted gathering-spaces, big as cathedrals, football grounds, shopping centres....'

'They *are* all those,' says Toma. 'They're not drains and sewers – they're where we'll live; our cities. All the metal, the stony stuff – is useless. Nickel is plating, gold is obsolete, iron rusts, you can't burn coal. Cobalt? You glow in the dark. This is our future, Milo....'

And he grips my arm – in fear, in hope. It's early yet, to say which sentiment prevails.

'The future,' Toma says. 'What we have hollowed out – it's still a secret. There's no parliaments been built, no roads to other places, no undergrounds, no bus or railway stations. "Elsewhere" is visible only on a screen....'

'I've been long arriving, Toma,' I say, 'at the truth. Today is everything, everything is today. Maybe it will come as you say – perhaps I'll still feel free and happy. Perhaps a tile will fall on my head, and I'll be dead.'

'The tile affair would not have authorship,' he says. 'It wouldn't count. Being on the list – that will. Maybe you'll feel less free, less happy – how'll you measure it?'

'Putting me on report,' I say, 'is shabby. And all these plans – laid down in silence! Emptiness, a space beneath our feet; out of the sunlight, into the cave...!'

'I could not dynamite you, Milo,' Toma says. 'I don't have solutions. You're on "hold", and I'm just a lower figure in the totem.'

He invites me to his home, before I leave: taking the bus out West, or East, perhaps.

There's bread, a can of sardines: 'We eat poor,' he says. 'It reminds us where we were, and what we left.'

It's meagre, but I take my fork, to spear at least a couple of the headless fish.... 'No,' he says. 'Grace! Milo, I know you have a relationship with God.... I've heard you talk. Remember the miracle – the fish, the bread ... perhaps there'll be a miracle again, and we'll be satisfied, without the massacre, the lambs, the goats, the ram – the thicket, remember ... family comes first ... as for the Philistines, the rest – eat poor and trust.... Those sardines will grow into dolphins, porpoises and whales....'

'Oh,' I say, 'don't get me wrong. I don't believe. If I say "God" – I mean Reason, like they had long long ago. A force; a plan, a purpose. A crazy driver full of self and hate, but an idiot who had – at least – a steering wheel. ... I kept – my impersonal faith in Being. God made a cranky universe, crumbling, a game of *Go,* a three card trick. Creating but immortal – a contradiction....'

'Quiet!' Toma says. 'My wife will say a grace.' And so she does.

I go on.... 'A puzzle you can solve in different ways. I have. I put the pieces back, in the box – you don't want to fiddle any more. It's finished, Toma, long ago. On to the next....'

'Be very very careful, Milo,' Toma says. 'I've put you on the list, you won't get off and all you do will fail, be made to fail before you even think that you might find a peaceful spot and rest....'

'Oh no,' I say. 'I don't want peace. There is no peace – there's floods.'

Toma ... the Beast.

The future – underground. Like Mister Tod, except – we'll all live in a mine, that's dug right out, immense.

*

There is no miracle – there's lots of bread, though; few sardines, though we are seven or eight, not counting the musicians. They don't play. That family does itself well – it's clearly worth one's while, to be a shift boss with a degree in dynamiting sciences.

*

'I shall need work, if I'm to survive,' I tell the woman, there in an office, paid to give advice.

'I'll give advice,' she says, 'but not a job. You're blacklisted – as you must suspect.'

'I'm hungry,' I tell her, embarrassed. 'There was no miracle again at dinnertime. And – believe me, I didn't want to make you all unfree. Have you reflect, maybe. Peek down to where the mining's done, perhaps.'

'You're quite persuasive,' Elina, the advisor, says, putting on her coat. 'I'll take you home and fill you up,' and so she does.

'Now,' she says, 'I want the garden cleared.'

'I'm not sure it's legal,' I say. 'It's immense, and tall. It makes a wonderful green light in here, like being in an aquarium, not being fish.'

'You're a poet, Milo,' Elina says. 'It's true, employing you may not be legal. I can't pay, and can't ask anyone – I'm the authority. What a bore. I long to be in an apartment, with no garden. I want this one all ploughed up, when you have cut it back. Some metres down, you'll find a Rototiller underneath, gassed up....'

'The stuff, Elina,' I ask. 'What do I do with it?'

'Nothing,' she says. 'I believe it will be dead. You know about gardening, I don't.'

'There could be rarities,' I say. 'Variants. Animals, and creeping things.'

'Use your initiative,' she says. 'I must go to work.'

If Nadine had made a movie about our ark, the story would have gyred around like this. From project to banality, restoration on a tiny scale.

The job – in essence it is easy. No politics, no secrets, are involved. It can be done: and satisfy.

There's tendrils reaching to the roof, some have forced their way under the tiles, into our room, there's moss inside the shower, a vigorous bignonia running up and down the stairs. All green and brown. A marvel.

I find a suitcase, fill it with her food, and leave. In distant times, you'd say she was a communist. She has the Plan. But now ... maybe she's against nature running free. On the right, reactionary? I don't much care.

*

'You're a tyro,' Kylian says. 'Never say you want work – you'll have to scoop up sulphur with your tongue. Say you've got too much to do, they'll have to wait.... Peps them up....'

Dolores, who's grown mightily since she was sewn in to her clothes – a beauty, full of promises you know she's not allowed to keep – says, 'Lay off, Kylian – Milo's honest. I bet his grandad did a '68, and passed it on.'

Ah! Another couple… marriage, the great mystery….

'I seek advice,' I say. 'Then, I don't follow it. Travelling almost everywhere, I've found the three types of humankind. The reasonable, the unreasoning, and the don't knows. Which, pray, are you?'

We laugh. 'This outfit,' says Dolores, 'is my past and present. I was a dancing sylph – then, with the dope, I started to explode....'

'Don't give yourself away, Dolores,' Kylian says, much annoyed. 'Showbiz is mystery island – if you leave, you must leave your body there. You smuggled yours – it grew. Alas, you left your brain back there, under the coca tree.... They don't tell you, when you start, it ends in tragedy. I live that every day: you think there's comeback, bigger than before.... We're ghosts, my dear....'

'Are you unquiet?' I ask. 'Evil fascinates me – and its consequences. A bum act....'

'The bus,' says Kylian. 'It made her vomit. Pills kept it down.'

'A season in hell,' Dolores says. 'I dwindled ... a dried-out pod. My clothes fell off – they had to sew me in. But – I'm still keen. I'm like Napoleon's soldiers – my side-arm's in the rafters, my blue coat mends the roof – but say the name, and off I'll go....'

'To another great defeat,' I add, though I ought not. 'Song and dance?'

'My poems,' says Dolores, 'with a group. I was a waif. Bitter-sweet, the warnings. Who will be spared? Risk? How to trust the waves when the raft's insecure, the shore is in sight, but there's rocks, big swell....'

'We were poor,' Kylian says. 'She wrote, and it went down well – timeless. Remember "dappled things..."? Or "Nature all wonder, all silence...." For us it was the theatre where "in vain always in vain, we await – Being, on gossamer wings". But – her original stuff: more vinegar, more sugar. Stirred well. A trip. Not bad. All happened, exactly as she said.'

'I'm interested, Kylian,' I say. 'Was it "bad things happen, get over them, forget and laugh" – or, "We deserve bad things, we'll be better – if we survive."'

'Oh, both those,' says Dolores. 'Who isn't moved, who doesn't have anxiety – who doesn't want to save the others?'

'I know,' I say. 'I'm not censorious. I wonder if you've found a way of going deeper, any way – not just walking round, kissing lovers, making connections, metaphors and such? Marcus Aurelius...? Those Chinese governors who ordered executions, then arranged the chrysanthemums on their desk...?'

'She was the best,' says Kylian. 'Now, Dolores has outgrown her envelope – but we don't change the songs. They'll still bring success. She wears her outfit, though she's bursting through – it is her luck, her talisman....'

'I thought you had excluded success,' I say. 'The public don't care what happens to you anyway ... although it's true, if you are the morose type, you can spend a life committed and intent – looking for what does not exist.... And who,' I ask, 'do you blame, if things go wrong?'

'Who does bad, you mean?' she says. 'Doing things, reacting to them, not reacting anyhow? That all gets sorted out, you know. Time. Built in to everything.'

'I think of Raskolnikov,' I say, 'trying to explain why he killed the old woman – the bedbug ... to be like Napoleon, to dare; being mad, a suicide, possessed by Satan.... And Sonya says, to him, he must go, confess at the crossroads, 'God will send you life again.' Is killing someone a self-murder...? The ancients fantasised all around....

'Without God, in a future without crossroads – where do you go? The penal settlement: redemption through suffering.... Do you put that in your show?'

'It would be a corpse,' Dolores says, and laughs. 'Remember the machine, the Designer, killing the condemned man, when "no sign was visible of the promised redemption" – "through the forehead went the point of the great iron spike".'

'You've studied,' I say. 'Not that it means a thing. You wobble on the crime, reject the sense of punishment.'

'Well,' says Kylian, suddenly protective. 'So we do. Other shows will put it in – we leave it out. We are in our time. We don't look for rehab in the penal colony. It rings false.'

'Didn't it always?' I ask. 'Isn't that the point?'

'It doesn't matter, probably,' Dolores says. 'Some deaths are punished – not those in the flood. They never were ... and everybody disappears. And everybody can appreciate my act.'

'I won't insist,' I say. 'I don't have answers, and the question – maybe it eludes me, maybe – there is none. It's cloudy, fluid – maybe it's a falsity to bring in love and faith. For me – that's it. But then again – if you can get away with what you do by citing conscience – it's a cop-out! Judgements on yourself are alibis. Easier than jail-time, that's for sure.'

'No crime here, friend,' says Kylian. 'If you're fishing for one: nothing, *nada,* zilch. We're clean as newborns.'

'That's why I wanted to discuss with you, and now you say the innocent aren't interested.... The guilty would be,' I say, 'but they're schtum. Like you.'

We laugh.

'You talk thick matter, Milo,' Kylian says. 'In the middle of your wildwood, there's a denser forest. You'll be glad to be black-listed – you won't need suffer in a job.'

'I know,' I say. 'I've come to seem like that. Voluble, and out of time. I'm used to games where other people play and risk their cash, don't just complain when they don't win. Once people talked, or shouted, anyway – went to the movies, read a book....'

'We didn't have your opportunities,' Dolores says.

'That's evidently so,' I say.

'Possession by the spirits,' Kylian says. 'What's your solution? Dolores goes back to the start, repeats. Wears early clothes, hoping they'll still fit.

'You need strength in your legs – if the spirit's banished, the route march will begin ... you can't shrug off the loneliness, abandonment, the ostracism ...'

'Kylian knows my spirit,' says Dolores. 'It's not yet climbed into him....'

'Stop!' I say. 'Forget the spirit, just for now. We were addressing crime and punishment.'

'I've been good from birth,' Dolores says. 'That makes me vulnerable. Kylian understands.'

'I started with the flood; reality. It seemed a punishment. What was the crime?' I ask.

'That's poetry,' says Kylian, 'but not the kind we do. To you it may seem easy: – it's your metaphysics. That has collapsed. Forget it. Help us, if you want. We're animals, my friend, we purr and churr – your questions have no answer, no significance. Curiosity is your spirit – it climbed aboard, it spurs you on, to the abyss, the cliff edge – the spirit, it has wings. You'll drop; the spirit flies away, infects and drives, rides to destruction – we're its horse. Don't let it mount you ... not good and bad, not why and how. Forget all that, don't drink from death's deep ladle....'

'I'd come with you,' I say, 'but I'm no use. Nor you to me.'

'Something went wrong with you, that's true, Milo,' Kylian says. 'You don't stick, don't stick to people. That's bad for you, but good for them. Maybe it's all pretence for you: seeking what you know's not there, and you'd not know it if you'd found it.'

'That's art,' I say. 'The unicorn among the trees – but in the undergrowth, there's evil beetles, swarming on board.'

'If you can bang a drum,' Dolores says, 'you're hired.'

*

'Success,' I say, as we wait to go on stage one day, 'Means you must plug in. Some years back, it was about moving up, assimilating into higher earnings – new spend, upgrading your habits. Then – the fashion was moving down – making do: with dirty deals, exotica, and losing referents. You – we – want to stay still... repeat a modest season, followed by a winter ... naturally cold.'

'You haven't understood,' says Kylian. 'Music arrives from nowhere, then it stays, like poetry. Fiddling with it – that's for critics. They tell you what you've done. We haven't seen those yet: it makes no difference at all.'

All that – must be code. Kylian frets, Dolores sits, a bottle of blue curaçao on the floor beside her. I have a shaman's drum, with rings all round, that tinkle.

I could devote my life to her, make her my career; her travels and her act. If she wins a prize – be there, and if she dies – furnish the clip of her, reciting.

'Am I recognisable?' she asks. 'They must recognise me, then they'll see what I might have seen....' Her white face has purple lines drawn on – then you see, it's just the light. Not pale, not purple.

'Don't hold it in, Dolores,' I say. 'Remember how they changed your blood and put you in the rattle, when you fell and couldn't rise. The noise – they'll want to hear that.'

'We don't have a noise-maker,' she says.

I shake my drum, and say – 'You run the numbers: ... 'the light ... going out,' 'I don't deserve to live ...' 'a '72 Impala bumps down the drive....' People attach to that, it shows you share something, your humanity. It's your quiddity. It isn't necessary – they can see you. You aren't a robot.'

'You mean it's trite, my act?' Dolores asks.

'I mean it's what you are, and how you join to them,' I say. 'It's nakedness – we all have that, under our clothes. All the invention, the screaming, the incest, being in a Philipine cancer ward – they glide through that, and then it's "my curled fist grips uncut amethysts," or "I am seawrack, I break upon the shore." It's your fantasy, but it sticks to them. You're there – human! It needs no emphasis....'

'OK,' says Kylian, 'we're on!'

The public clings to Dolores, like they did ten years or more before. Her style ensures it.

She sings, chants, concludes – 'Love ... is a solitary thought ...' There's a pause, they applaud.

She must have heard Pierrot Lunaire done well – by a jazz singer.

People want to hear about love, the word spoken and sung. Crime is perhaps more interesting. Punishment – no one wants that.

Kylian – where was he, doing what, in those ten, fifteen years? Lots of solitude, lots of love even in a year: all passing, quick forgotten; white noise, white experience. Ups and downs, good times, bad times, and times.

'It went well,' I tell her. 'Yes,' she says.

'You put the brakes back on before we all did,' she says to me, when Kylian has given us each a small share of the takings. 'Raw emotions, no masks – those were the days! Now, we're under a tarpaulin. Gastronomy and exercise.'

'I hold back so as not to do bad by anyone,' I say.

I don't believe you can do much bad to people close to you....

'You think I made Kylian suffer?' Dolores asks.

'You should ask Kylian the same thing,' I say. 'Then try to put the answers together.'

'Oh, I wasn't with Kylian all this time. He went to be a biker. I wanted someone who would help me, not a sponsor,' she says.

It's true of everyone, I guess, though not of me.

*

'If you believe, you should go fight for it,' Kylian says.

Banging the drum is rather little to have me count as a musician, to get a sideman's rate.

'You need lots of belief or lots of poverty to go and fight,' I say. 'I'm not sure fighting fits what I am interested in. I think it might be the contrary to it.'

*

Dolores has an angle – not just on performance, but on all the rest: on life. I hang around her and Kylian, peering into their relationship: it seems quite dumb.

'That's it!' One evening, Dolores says, 'I knew I'd been successful. I shan't continue, there's no point. No more shows: finished! Give them their money back, Kylian. As for the band – we're black, not unionised. We don't owe anybody anything.'

'Successful?' I ask, amazed. 'You think it's just because of you, your egotism, your notions. What about the drumming and the presentation?'

'That's jealousy,' says Kylian. '*Invidia*: a mortal sin. You pass the time, Milo, saying you want to be useful. You're too late. You want a piece of what everybody has – a piece of pieces. The time that passes – you ask, what colour does it have, what taste? You could jump in and have sex with it. Everybody tries it.'

Dolores has been snipped out of her envelope; I see she's wearing Kylian's colours....

'Now I can be properly with Kylian,' she says.

'I've not known either of you – only your hopes,' I say. The most communicating part.

'I could go higher,' says Dolores.

It's true, absolutely true.

'You've been too cerebral, Dolores,' I say.

It falls flatly, sounds quite snobby.

'You're a driver, Milo,' says Dolores. 'You lack intensity.'

She laughs, I don't.

'I don't need to speed away,' I say. 'I never killed anyone. But I've been present at many deaths. Some imminent, some uncounted. You turn away before you get there, Dolores. You've no conclusion.'

'I try to be original,' she says. 'Things inevitable – don't interest me.'

'All that's left's embroidery, I fear,' I say.

I don't fear at all – fear's the only thing that I don't fear.

'You'll always fly higher than Kylian,' I say. 'Think very carefully what you mean to him, and he to you. Yours is a big sacrifice .... yourself. It's the only one you can think of making, though.'

We leave it there. I didn't deserve the job; nor being fired from it.

*

Mikhail is partly Russian.

'You're never partly Russian,' he says.

He speaks of his family as if he is an exile, with a reactionary policeman for brother, at home and prosperous. He treats me as privileged, undeserving, and, so, underpayable. It doesn't fit.

'Everywhere is going reactionary,' I say. 'Or to the lawyers.'

'It's a phase,' says Mikhail. 'There's no other phase.'

I persist. 'I have this authoritarian streak,' I say. 'It troubles me, more than my anarchic streak.'

'Authority? You have to get things done,' he says. 'Line up the tumbrils. Then repent – set all the headless ones to walk around again.'

Larissa, his lover, helps us.

We all met at Dolores' after-show. Everyone there had wanted to be met.

Mikhail and I run campaigns for political prisoners. We knew nothing about them, but we had followers, and we were watched and hassled. By cops, spooks, anyone at all. Thousands of them.

'What do you need to know about political prisoners?' Mikhail would ask. 'It's enough that's what they are.'

We got money from people who wanted to spend surplus cash while they were alive, not leave it to a proper charity.

Larissa kept a kind of archive, and pretended she wasn't the motor of the enterprise.

'I don't want to die in this office, Mikhail,' I said.

'Then collect the rags to bind your feet for when the column reaches the tundra,' he says. 'Your boots will be useless by then.'

He too wants something different. I think he wants to be a personality.

'Prisoners of risk,' says Larissa: 'Conscience is that: politics is not.'

Mikhail and I – we're superficial, but totally committed to the prisoners. We're one step back, of course – otherwise you're on the rope with them, and fall together when you try to grab them. Being superficial, we were under surveillance, but not so well informed we had to walk the rope above the void. Larissa knew the serious side, the consequences. Mikhail and I – we didn't. Didn't believe anything could happen to us, how easy it was to be entrapped, how many tricksters were enveigling us.... We two were the only ones who thought we were completely innocent, and so we went on, daring.

Larissa does the politics – Mikhail – the imprisonment part....

'It's confinement,' says Larissa. 'Mikhail was imprudent, did a little time. You never knew – if they would let you go, or when they took you out – what would it be? And you,' she asks me, 'where do you fit in?' She cuddles me, to show her question has a critical point, but I'm forgiven for what I haven't done and what I'm not, and being trusting and ingenuous. I hug her back, for what there will not be.

*

'No one in power likes opposition,' Mikhail says. 'The old colonial powers exported their repression. Now, they've changed their tack: making stuff and selling it abroad. Interfering, exhorting, giving business and a litle cash. Tolerance? Up to a point, at home. Poor states get tough, the rich rely on them to keep the peace and keep their problems to themselves. If troubles start to spill into the metropolis – then there's a call to arms.

'We have in front of us – a sea of shipwrecked people, struggling in the waves, trying to get to shore. We have no boat, no rope. We shout, that's all. There seem more people drowning than there can be waves to hold them – and what do we have in hand? Me and Larissa.

'And you, Milo, are you around because you're chocolate, soft and sweet, and don't know what else to be?'

*

'Those religions – they're the icebergs. They can't change – they're born in a particular way, alas – without a brain, but they grow big and hairy, they whoop and climb up in the trees....' Larissa says, and laughs as she slips off her metaphors, nearly drops into the sea herself – 'They melt, become tsunamis. Their belief – is poetry,' she says. 'The real people, with a chance to act, decide – they give us rhetoric! Look in the jails, dear Milo, see who's got the key. Politics: states and conmen. We must be very very careful.... Behind the small determined powers, there's big determined ones....'

'I guess then,' I say, being very very careful, 'you select our prisoners, Larissa? Those we back?'

'Of course,' she says. 'Some guys, I hope they rot inside.'

'Those you – we – back,' I say. 'What happens?'

'Some get a trial, some die, some do a deal, and others disappear,' she says. 'It's politics. When a regime doesn't jail its opposition, they have someone somewhere else put the inconvenient guys inside.... Sometimes – it's generalised, and there is a global tide. One way or another, we are all inside ... or soon shall be.'

'Well,' I say, amazed by the complexity. 'Do we do good? Does somebody?'

'Of course we do, my dear,' she says. 'Being shut up is seldom nice, especially if you've not done what you're banged up on suspicion that you did....'

'What?' I ask. 'What is the doing that takes us to the heart....'

'We aren't a power,' she says. 'It's powers that can decide. What matters is – our intention is a good. Be content. That goodness is more than you have ever been a party to before.... My answer to your questioning is all you're going to get.'

'But do we want justice, or just – laws?' I ask.

'I want our followers to feel they're satisfied,' she says. 'And that they're clean. I want Mikhail. I want to keep us out of jail. As for the rest – the balance is between more power and less dissent: or no power, anarchy – doing what you want. You see – apparently it's quite a split....'

'I see that,' I say. 'So, what do *we* want?'

'Mikhail tends to anarchy. I'm the type who's orderly. I don't trust people – that's my creed. If we could trust them, we'd not need campaign. Mikhail's anarchy is what we had before. States build on anarchy, they're the remedy and then the cause; they need it, stop it, institute it. Anarchy brings power, confers and calls for it, it concentrates in cells and execution yards ... I could love anarchy, but it creates the horrors, and to avoid the horrors it produces, you get order, horror permanent.'

'I see,' I say. 'So – make everywhere like here? Half and half?'

'No, no,' says Mikhail. 'That means infinite wars. Besides – no one likes equality. Before, there were infinite wars for the rich to keep the inequality. Now, it takes a different form. You lose an empire, then to build again, you have to share the power – and hope the battles can be kept outside: outside your home. Wars for justice? Avoid them! We're more modest, Milo ... we accept the situation as it is. We keep the temperature down.

'Capitalism? Rather than the cause, it is the vehicle that shifts power round: once discovered, it will always be more revolutionary than the wheel! Jailing guys – is trouble in the long term. In the short – it just corrodes. Accept it, Milo, reality, and the little we can do....'

'I do, I do,' I say, I think. Mikhail, Larissa – they don't believe I have understood.

They start to watch me, like the others do.

*

'Most Russians,' Mikhail says, 'have never seen a wolf. They mostly don't drive sleighs. But everybody knows that wolves take care of innocents. A child falls in the snow – they take it in, and it stays part of us, becomes a part of them.'

'Forget the sugar, Mikhail,' says Larissa, grimly. 'Milo! We need to throw you off the sled. The wolves have very nicely asked....'

'I understand,' I say. 'Why me?'

'That's what you shouldn't ask,' she says. 'Best welcome your new family: those waving tails, the songs, the love ... all things you lacked in human life....'

'We made an error, Milo,' Mikhail says. 'Forget the wolves – I know experience with the animals has stayed with you and twisted your cosmology.... The problem is – we didn't know, one of our prisoners is a shit.... More properly – an evil person. Maybe an evil one among the evil many, paid and persuaded to be so – fear and hubris, love and hate.... All the emotions and their skews.... We must retreat, admit an error, throw someone off the sleigh, not to become a wolf-child, but, alas, my friend, be eaten raw....'

I am aghast. 'Who made you renege on this, Mikhail, your plan? A state? A person who you seem to trust? If we retreat, it throws a darkness on all attempts to save these guys from voids and tortures.... It implies we're stupid, ignorant. Or in the grip of some political power. The whole project shudders, ends in shadow and in doubt....'

'We can't discuss all this with you,' Larissa says, cutting Mikhail off. 'We never promised justice, not to anyone – in fact, we quite mistrust it.... Justice is power, maybe supreme, and that we cannot countenance. Justice stands behind injustice, the power replacing, standing on, perhaps embracing, its twin, injustice ... blind justice is effectively injustice: that's a lesson I have taught....'

'So,' I say, 'I am the sacrifice? I'm to be consumed? And all the rest, our prisoners....'

'To save them, Milo,' Mikhail says, wringing his hands, brushing some tears, 'you must take the honourable step. For us, yes – it's dishonour, but to survive, we have no choice. It's life, my friend: you've often said life's good, worth preserving, up to a point. Remember that, and pack your stuff....'

*

I say to Larissa, 'You mean – I take the blame for your mistake. I'm fired. The guy goes back out of our light, into the shade.... Who imposes that? I understand some innocent must pay, and that it can't be you.... But who has used their power? Is there a truth? A lie? Who has to suffer? Why?'

'We're not a cure,' Larissa says. 'We are a palliative, and those are excellent, if you're in need. The states who feel they're stable – they promote us, in a way. Opposition strengthens stable states. We do no harm to them.

'We light up the prisoners – for them, it's a big deal. For states it doesn't stir a leaf. It's delicate for us....'

'Which state?' I ask. 'Who told you to back off, and won't they always try?'

She smiles. 'What do you want from me, Milo? Sex? A contract?'

'Yes,' I say. 'Both, for a start.'

'You must be careful now,' she says. 'You've become an outlaw. A dupe and liar, partisan. A meddling fraud, expendable. In the service....'

'Yes,' I say. 'At least tell me whose service....'

'It won't help,' she says. 'All services are secret, and what they know are secrets too.'

'Who set me up?' I insist.

'You're insignificant,' she says.

'Then whose is the plot? Yours? Someone else's?' I ask. 'Is this all I'll ever know?'

'Take it as a lesson into good and bad,' she says.

MALEK. SOMETIME EMPLOYER OF CASUAL LABOUR

I wonder who the prisoner was.

'No one will want you now,' says Malek. 'You're a suspect. What you might have wanted – you won't be able....'

'I've been curious,' I say. 'That's all.'

'That's enough,' he says. 'Seek the company of other outlaws. That's the best for you.'

'I understand,' I say. 'Maybe it was standing aside: the seals? Or the Touareg, Issouf. Or friends – Dolores? Or more likely Kylian.... Those bikers – reactionaries, for sure. Or was it trying to get freedom for Maisoon? – someone was irritated.... Then there's the mine... Kemal, anyone, a friend or enemy could have been promised something to bring my cadaver in....'

'None of it sounds serious, Malek says. 'Don't fall into paranoia. The point is – there's a pattern. You're the storm-cock, Milo. Everybody's quiet but you. Everybody's taken cover long ago – it's yours, the voice in the stillness.... Warning when everybody's warned.'

'No voice, Malek,' I say. 'A croak.'

'If you do wrong,' he says, 'you go to court. If you *are* wrong – there's no one.'

'I reached no conclusion,' I say. 'Conclusions come without my say.'

'Too many names,' he says. 'Not from your street. A swarm of them. You've built up risks....'

‘I’ll find some outlaws,’ I say. ‘Get odd jobs from them.’

‘I’m beyond the law,’ he says. ‘All these antiquities are false –’ and he points to boxes full of broken stuff.

‘You can’t make them now to look the same as if they’re old. The genuine are stolen – but not from anyone. The new are better than the old, better made, and more complete. They’re what the ancients had in mind. Both kinds are good and true. It’s better to copy than to steal.... I have no work for you, Milo....’

‘I can’t follow you, Malek,’ I say. ‘What’s the distinction between old and new? Price? The collector’s mania? The myth of authenticity: as if an object has a spirit....’

‘Oh, it does,’ he says. ‘Of course it does. Don’t you? – your sagging body’s not worth chaff without one. *Geist;* your ghost.’

It’s a cold thought. He watches me freeze. ‘Who’s been after you? It doesn’t matter. What matters is your life, being alive to live it through,’ he says. ‘I have the faith. You don’t – it’s an error.’

‘Faith in what?’ I ask. ‘A book? A voice from long ago?’

‘Faith in anything I want,’ says Malek. ‘Spirits, work, amnesty; the great change, the animals waving at the sun.... You don’t have faith, Milo. That’s one result of persecution of a normal kind – the result’s the worst part. Consequences always are.’

'My suspicion, then,' I say, 'is right. That bad luck isn't innocence, isn't chance at all, not empty vessels in a void that clash, bad thoughts and bad intentions making a contact, live wires that enter at your heel and reach the heart.... It's people ganging up. Against me, and everyone. For what, though? Futility!

'Tell me, Malek, what does all this signify?'

'I'm convinced,' he says. 'It's the imaginative life of brains, humanity's ability to imagine what is not; the abstract. It's white noise and sound, like a radio emits when there is nothing, no one there. Something, some signal – there always is. If there were significance, perhaps we'd hear a story that we're in but isn't quite as reasonable, connected as it seems it ought to be.... It's just the mind's capacity, Milo. It isn't useful, isn't functional – it always works and grinds, a mechanism that has not been connected up, that moves, revolves, but isn't productive, not of anything....'

'It's what inventions, memories come from,' I say.

'Maybe,' he says. 'But that's my point. We're stuck at the beginning, in bodies primitive, our project impossible. We're not up to it. Inventions haven't changed the species, memories aren't good, they're bad. And they're useless, except to remember what is poisonous and what's not.'

'This is more drastic than I want,' I say. 'I'll do you an inventory. See what you abandoned guys might need. I won't buy your lumps of clay and rust. Or listen to your speculations....'

'Not rust,' he says. 'Where our civilisation ended, it had gone beyond the rusting. Corrosion had begun ... an obsolescence....'

I say, 'I don't accept this, Malek: it's saying there is no refinement, no improvement....'

'The good part,' Malek says, 'is that the imaginary produces hums and chords, disconnected pictures, without significance, without a continuity. But – you are still here! Unbound: not contracted to a good or bad, not to a monster, not to an angel. You're irrelevant, I'm sure, but....'

I understand his argument.

'You mean – I have more time,' I say. 'Time for anything.'

'Beware,' he says. 'Looking for good and bad – it's all deception. The angel wants to change you, possess you, master you. The monster's good – it only wants to eat you – and after all, you can eat her.'

*

The people here, enduring war and weather, famines and inflation, deportations and invasion –

'I can calculate your needs, the risks to you and me,' I say, 'and then I write it down, and someone else decides what you will get....'

'You're a castaway, you mean?' he asks. 'Not with an organisation....'

'I'm sure my contacts....' I begin.

'Do as you're trained,' he says. 'To have been dumped here means you've no resource.'

'In mathematics,' I go on, 'chance is incalculable. Good and bad: if they exist, many people don't agree with which is what, and many don't distinguish. I've made a good start on the mysteries, though, the "things of life"....'

'Maybe love still eludes you,' Malek says. 'That's where most people start.'

'Is there danger here?' I ask, hurrying him along ... love and sex are like good and bad – and there's no ark big enough and caulked so that it holds all their varieties....

'Here,' he says, 'the troubles passed. There's potshots and kidnaps, holdups too – but those you find all over. Food is promised in a year....' He laughs. I don't know if that is a joke.

There's sheds, the lids locked down – a rattle and a clang inside, it isn't dwarves, I guess, and they're not making golden rings – 'Bike frames and sneakers, tires and such,' he says. 'We suffer that, then we get rich, and pass it on.....

'Over there –' and he points to a line of clouds, beneath, a hazy range of hills; we feel a breeze insistent and the sound of hammers fades.

'Over there,' says Malek, 'China lies. One day, we shall go in, be welcomed, see the splendours they've imagined – light-shows, I'm sure, that cover over all the modern stuff, and take you back to Ming and Tang....'

'Shall we get in?' I ask. 'Without a question?'

'You like questions, Milo,' Malek says. 'But I don't expect they'll give you answers.'

'Before we try,' I say, 'I'm interested in the guy, the prisoner, whose history changed my life, and had Larissa send me here....'

'Oh,' Malek says. 'Some countries, they're all political prisoners. And in the end, some places reach a point where there's no politics at all – you take best offer, or you stay at home, believe anything, and say you're sceptical. Free! From politics...!

'Your prisoner – is a dry leaf clinging to a tree that sprouts dry leaves. Are they a traitor? A corrupter, a corrupted? It won't surprise me, and it shouldn't disturb you.... In our world, nothing is exaggerated, nothing is unique or beyond reason ... no belief, no action – excess or stasis, each is equally capable of either....'

'I know, I know,' I say, impatiently. 'It's the specific interests me. Don't say "all and none's specific" ... you're a runester – all's indecipherable, all can mean anything at all.'

'It's a technique that prisoners learn,' he says. That finishes it.

'It's beautiful here, don't you see?' he asks. 'With all the houses gone.'

'There's the rubble, I say, 'And weeds.'

'No one at all,' he says. 'You can see – someone had an idea, for something new. Totally new. They call it "late style" – if it is late. "Style" anyway, could come from anywhere. Graeco-Arab. Thai-Malay. There's a saying, "It don't mean a thing, if you ain't got that style."'

'I hadn't heard that,' I say. 'You must have had hard times. During the wars.'

'You too,' he says. 'Not on your head, but ways off, maybe overseas. Those places – Aden, Algeria, al-Basrah – right down your alphabet.'

'I wasn't born,' I say. 'They waited till they'd settled those, before they had me.' It's a joke, if not a rollicking one.

'You must think this is a dirty place,' says Malek, 'and left us dirty, being here. To survive you must make compromises, join the dance, this crowd and that. And in the end – I've suffered more than you.'

'Maybe you have,' I say. 'Now, you're on a pleasant interlude with me. I haven't suffered for myself, not at all: I suffer for other people: through them.'

'It doesn't count,' says Malek. 'Suffering can't be vicarious.'

'It's not a competition, Malek,' I say, irritated. 'There's no way to judge, no point, in who is suffering more. Since Maisoon, I've not thought of a relationship – you take on so much weight ... a couple, all is multiplied. The more you take on, the more stories started, abandoned, you're found wanting: the less you want to go on and repeat the ritual....'

'Things are looking up for me,' he says, not listening. 'But I foresee – they're worsening for you. You face a stormy time, my friend.'

'Let's do what we have to do,' I say. 'Find the prisoner, see who did right, and wrong, and why I took the blame.'

'They bombed the jails,' he says. 'To let the people out. The prisons were imposing here, with many floors, and offices above. The cells are underground, and with the upper part collapsed – the prisoners can't get out.'

'I know,' I say. 'That's not the point. A prisoner, it seems, did not deserve our help. Maybe an informer, or a plant.... A common criminal – that's what they're called; perhaps an agent. A renegade, a terrorist, a boss.... Someone in the regime – a big name, a vendetta....'

'Strange it interests you,' Malek says. 'What matters isn't a prisoner, it's Larissa making the mistake. She needs to cover what she did, that's all. You're not here on a quest, Milo, you're here to disappear.'

He laughs and laughs.

*

'What's that?' I ask.

An immense pile of ruddy sand.

'It's a tunnel,' Malek says. 'It's why we're both here. It's not exactly future: it's a plan that I can write you into – and myself. We hoped for a tunnel beneath the sea – to America! It was not to be. Now, it could be China. We'll have to work on it – sand is hard to tunnel under, but it brings us work. We won't go to China, Milo, this path will be one-way. But you've not suffered, not enough – you don't grasp reality, the transformations. You have piles of realities yet to come. You might join these guys ... you're useless but you're curious. That is your gift. How do we tunnel, have the grains stick long enough....'

There's a band of men, with shovels, sitting on the sand, peering at contracts in Mandarin.

'Why are we here, Malek?' I ask. 'If you're not the prisoner, maybe you're a guard?'

'Ask the canary,' says Malek, 'who's in the cage? It all depends where your horizon ends – and that doesn't depend on you, it's the design. The spatial context.'

'Maybe we should help those guys,' I say. 'Read their contracts.'

'I don't know the writing,' Malek says. 'The numbers are Arabic – they seem very high. To read – you need undo the character, go back to the basics, then imagine, how you or any sapient human, could start from simplicity, and reassemble.... From the concrete comes the concept – not with a name, a bundle of fresh shoots. It's not easy, it's not the way you work, Milo, and yet – the mind, constructing, is not alien. It's not as hard as crosswords – it is you that's become more difficult....'

‘Look,’ I say, ‘that must be a Union Hall. There’ll be a meeting, to examine what’s being written. It’s their future...’

‘Our future,’ Malek says. ‘All those who have an interest, who think they have a future, and know they have a past still lying here.... We’re us in stages – Manchus and Turks, the Gobi, Anatolia ... then the Danube, the Carpathians.... You, Milo, you and the Mongols who went almost everywhere, even the Americas, where they’d arrived a thousand years before, and started building empires, with cosmologies among the most intricate there’s ever been, and landed on each planet, but very delicate and careful, not leaving germs and footprints, no car-crash piles of aluminium. Then left, closing the door quietly, locking up – as if they’d never been, no boasting and no flags....’

We contemplate. It’s very sad and philosophical. He points to the geodesic dome before us, says –

‘You can see the motto, “Love one another, and die”. It must be from the Qur’an, a book I promise I would read in my spare time ... learn, follow, in my spare time too, perhaps; if I reach retirement, if I know what I can retire from....’

‘No tears, Malek,’ I say. ‘See – the Greens have a picture on a loop – it’s reindeers in a circle, round and round in thousands – it’s like the pilgrims wheeling round the satanic stone in Mecca, except in the middle there’s no stone, there’s a reindeer, or a caribou – whatever is the difference; it’s bewildered, central quite by chance, and all of them incapable of wanting to be something else....'

'That, you cannot know,' he says, 'though you might imagine it. Going on a pilgrimage so's to be good – it's a beginning, though if this is a Union Hall, there haven't been unions for quite a while; and being something else, or even what you are – it's not the fashion. Here, they'll be discussing futures ... your future, mine; and some will be in finance, and looking into futures that are real....'

There's a platform, with some wizened guys sat there, turning their heads slow, deliberate, like tortoises, and sometimes – are there jokes, something risqué or shocking, some piece of scandal? – they put their hands on their faces, covering their eyes, their mouths, their dried apricot ears....

'Wise monkeys, Malek,' I say, keeping my sound down, but out it comes, a blart of giggle. 'They're people I was at school with, or who look like them. Who'd have said they'd done so well, and me so bad?'

'Oh,' says Malek, laughing too, but silently, 'that wasn't at all hard to tell. But – these guys, don't look like labour lawyers, nor as if they understand an ideogram. They must be into futures properly, your future, mine, that you can swear by. I hope it's not all platitudes and hope and warnings.... Getting those grains of sand to stick, so you can drive a train or truck beneath them – that is mighty hard.'

'These wise men,' I say, 'they don't seem to me to be union guys. If they don't have the answers, maybe they hope you have some clues. Go up and tell them, Malek!'

'Those images,' he says, staying firmly put. 'The caribou.... What's the difference here, my friend, under this scalding sun, between an image and a mirage?'

'Yes!' I say. 'That's a nice one, a beauty, Malek. Ask the guys at the head table!'

He's delighted. 'Your school friends!' he says. 'Who knew so much more than you, when all your minds were fresh and empty! Ask too about sticking the sand together, like it once was, and making gardens here, green, with pineapples and kumquats ... The animals that feed on them ... and us that feed on those.... Those old wise guys – maybe they could make us paradise, and when they've done that, a mushroom stew with pine nuts, chick peas, like my mother didn't make.'

'You're droll, Malek,' I say, 'but you've led me here – I don't know which side all this is on, and why. The gurus up there seem listless, and the guys in the hall – they wander in and out, they cheer and sleep ... there's screwing indiscriminate, strumming of ouds, scraping of tars....'

'I know,' says Malek, turning solemn. 'As a playmate, I'm ambiguous. I don't provide you with what you hope for – a wife, a *Liebling*, who gives and gives and loads herself on you, like a bucketful of coal. Hot: smoky.

'The only one who ever loves you for yourself, is you. And you know, you are not lovable.'

'There must be a contract, Malek,' I say, ignoring him. 'Even if we can't read it, we must have a future, as one, or as multitudes. That's what a contract is about.'

We wait. There's music, someone sings a sad song and is hushed. The gurus leave the stage.

A crate of doves is brought.

Malek says, 'They'll let them go – they hover round, there's not the food they recognise.... They'll look for water, possibly....'

I cannot weep – everyone's worse off than me, or probably. We're not told anything.

*

Back the wise monkeys come: the chief one stands, and shouts, 'It's been decided. Everyone will get a contract. The meeting's over. Go in peace.'

'And is that good?' I ask Malek. 'The guys seem pleased....'

'That's because we can all go home,' says Malek. 'You can't, of course – you're on a mission. Don't be hard on your Larissa. You aren't good with women, Milo – you expect too much and don't give anything. Larissa makes mistakes, and probably you're one – she gave you much to do.... 'Root out injustice – don't be taken in. Don't be denounced.' And remember, she has a soft spot for the innocent.'

'I understand. I'm ready, Malek,' I say, eager and alert. 'It's just I don't know what it is I have to do.'

'That's why she appointed me, as your guide,' he says. 'Tell me where you want to go, I'll guide you.'

'I'll need protection, Malek. There's people here with uniforms and arms – are they for me, or against?' I ask.

'Don't be an ass,' he says. 'It all depends. We all know that.'

'Just being here,' I say, 'has answered questions. The monkeys, especially. The tunnel – imagine, the dinosaurs would have walked round, or over ... to anywhere – but not the Gulf of Mexico....'

We laugh. 'The dinos – they were heavy, but they travelled light,' he says. 'Soon, we shall receive instructions directly in our ears – and then we'll know the consequences of what we do before we even think of doing it. And we'll surpass them, our scaly ancestors. Our meteorology will be the tops – we'll sense the rain of ash before it falls.... '

'It won't resolve the problems I have faced,' I say, anxious not to alienate him. 'But I know what to do so's I'm not caught....'

'The pity is,' he says, 'you can't go back and do things in a better way. Knowledge is not retroactive – and,' he whispers, 'it isn't valid for tomorrow either.'

'There's no cure for regret,' I say. 'It's irreversible.'

'Let's gather strength, before we start the next stage,' Malek says, sitting on a pile of sand, prising out the grains between his toes.

*

'I have the dead all round me,' I say. 'Dead, disappeared, or missing in inaction – mine. I should have done much more to help the seals....'

About the author

John Fraser lives near Rome. Previously, he worked in England and Canada.

www.ingramcontent.com/pod-product-compliance
Lightning Source LLC
Chambersburg PA
CBHW020549310726
48979CB00008B/1149/J

* 9 7 8 1 9 1 4 9 3 8 0 6 1 *